The Twilight

And Other Tales

The Twilight
And Other Tales

Hermann Stehr

K A Nitz
LOWER HUTT

Das Abendrot first published 1901,
Das letzte Kind first published 1905,
Die Geschichte vom Rauschen
first published 1902, and
Der Schatten first published 1905

These translations by Kerry Nitz
Copyright © K A Nitz 2013
All rights reserved

ISBN: 978-0-473-24447-7

National Library of New Zealand Cataloguing-
in-Publication Data

Stehr, Hermann, 1864-1940.
The twilight and other tales / by Hermann
Stehr ; translated by
Kerry Nitz.
ISBN 978-0-473-24447-7 (pbk.)—ISBN 978-
0-473-24448-4 (MOBI)
I. Nitz, K. A. (Kerry Alistair), 1971- II. Title
833.912—dc 23

Contents

The Twilight

The heavy singing of the nearby mountain forest in which the evening wind was starting to awake floated through the open door of the little room and perished there into a sound which, like the dragging of steps wandering past, rang out dispersed over short intervals and vanished ghostlike — without stopping, like an audible vibration of the air.

Old Mrs Wiesner stood by the repaired, brown tiled range and was about to take a pot with boiling beets from the stove. At this sound, mysteriously drawn in from outside, she let her hand with the dirty stove cloth fall.

The restless, monotonous tapping of her husband rang out from the dim adjoining room. A grumpy, stooped old man, he was turning between his spread knees a half-finished basket made of green canes, grumbling constantly.

"Give the tapping a rest for once!" the gaunt old woman said and stroked her white hair into her headscarf, the white hair which was dry and brittle like the dying grass of dry plateaus.

Her gaunt fingers, warped by work, then skimmed hesitantly down her hollowed temples. When she had thus come in trembling touches close to the sharp cheekbones of her face, this intermittent dragging again wandered into the room from outside, and the tips of her brown fingers pressed into the wrinkles of her withered skin, as if they could thereby increase the sharpness of her hearing. Her eyes widened at the same time and a shimmering desire appeared in her tired eyes.

The old man's hammer drummed heedlessly on the canes.

"Be quiet for once with the damned racket!" she nagged at her husband crossly and took half a step to the right so that she partly faced the door into the adjoining room.

"You, you should be quiet!" she repeated in increasing agitation when the tapping did not break off. "You — don't you hear it?!"

Crossly, Wiesner finally let go of the basket and raised his head a little, listening.

Then it was quite silent.

"Well, what is it then? — — — damned dawdling, that!"

With that he burrowed thrusting with his left hand in his beard, which as a thick entanglement took up his entire face with the exception of his forehead and a small part of his cheeks, and his nose also protruded out of it. Thus his head, standing out against the light from the window opposite, had quite an animal-like outline.

"Now — I've had enough of this joke! — What could it be?" he concluded after dully pondering for a while.

"Listen up! Isn't it somebody walking off in the distance ... someone coming? ... long strides ... quite, probably quite in the distance, but yet in our house ..."

These words by his wife made the man listen attentively again.

"Oh, my God! — yes, yes, yes, if it could be! — Certainly, certainly; dammit! ...... but, how many are there?"

His wife's hands sank down, and her right hand kept grasping at the dirty stove cloth.

"You, my God," she started from her hidden thoughts, "I'd rather not look first ..."

"Well yes, of course, if it is nothing again?"

"... truly, it goes on constantly quite far off, as if someone is coming and not wanting to arrive, as if they were shuffling with every step, dead tired ... what use is the hour, what use is it? — — it is half past five."

"Guste will be having a haul on the schnaps — haha — it'll be going nicely — haha — he has to swill one down of course ... he likes to, he likes to! — if it is and he would be going just nicely ..."

Mrs Wiesner sat down on the chair next to the door.

After a long time raptly listening, the words came softly from her,

"Oh well and even if it was all just the forest, all of it, even the walking — it is all the same."

Wiesner did not understand her and directed his eyes at her knees which protruded a little past the doorposts and moved jerkingly so that they always knocked against each other.

"Why are you waggling your legs?" he asked.

"They waggle by themselves," she answered absentmindedly.

"Oh my God too, and me first," the man lamented with mournful fury, "if I went and heaved my two sticks just so far away, I'd have to try again, I'd have to go along on my knees after them. — Yes. — And that I'd have for all its trouble."

"Yes, yes, our misfortune is from hard work and the poverty from slaving away."

"Jesus, you country goose, such words! — It would probably have gone well, if he hadn't shot himself. He would have ordered us the heavy rest, he would have gifted us the seeds, the wood would have cost us nothing, I wouldn't have paid any interest. Why couldn't it have gone so?"

"Go!"

"Well yes, go! What else would you want?"

"Go! — Go! — Go!! — Doesn't it go *now*?"

"Oh well, what then, dammit, what do you want then, wife, what are you hollering?" —

The deepest torment burrowed into the face of the gaunt old woman.

Then she answered roughly, almost unintelligibly,

"Because you're talking to me ... that first time ... and because now it is too late ..."

Wiesner turned his head around astonished. He looked at her sharply, as many years ago a cane springing back had struck out his left eye.

He observed her thoughtfully for a long time in this stooped posture.

"You, Hanne!" he startled his wife, "would I be responsible for everything? — You think about it! — Wasn't I a coachman like a prince! — The six hundred taler that I was paid at the time, hey, was that something for you? — Didn't I use everything that was left with the head forester! — My God too, I wasn't a fool either; and everything with fairness and equity. God's gift must be honoured. What spoils with a rich man should rescue the poor man from his misery ..."

"Man, stop!" Hanne interrupted him.

"Well, I should tell, dammit!"

"It's perhaps better you'd said nothing."

She stared motionless at the floor. Her white, dead wisps of hair just trembled softly.

Then she straightened up, shoved her hair into her headscarf and looked for a long time and attentively through all the windows in turn so as to finally speak to herself,

"Now it's closed again."

"What is, what's closed again?"

"Oh, you don't see anything."

"Well yes! — Hmhm — dammit! All of it, blind sod, right, I'll ..."

He yelled out shrilly and grasped at his stick from old habit, but then remembered his ailment and desisted from it with groans.

"And if you rage at me too, the gap still won't open for you," she replied to his not misunderstood movement and concluded, torn up again by the whirl of her longing, "And it won't be closed to me today ... it is probably the end."

Then she tossed the cloth away as if she was thereby shedding the torment of her entire life, and spread her arms out as though in yearning for flight,

"It is always wandering around the house — and yet never comes in. As long as it was still just wandering, as he shot himself ... and I believed too, then everything could be right again."

"Wife, mad ...!" her husband prodded at her roughly and with scorn.

She let her arms sink and stood quietly and attentively like an artful child.

But already after a few moments, as though driven by the inexorable urge of a thirst, she was cherishing the images of her soul. She stepped quickly to the door of the adjoining room so that the old man raised his head even more at such audacity, and she looked at him for a long time with a sympathy which breathed a shimmer of childishness into the wrinkles of her face.

"Time is like a wall, and our fortune goes back and forth behind it," she began a deep play of hidden thoughts. "Just children and lovers see it going. But whoever isn't dead in life hears it going between day and night and night and day, but loudest of all when your end calls ..."

"I think you are hearing that Guste boy," Wiesner interrupted and looked at her disappointedly and with a soft tremor in his face.

This interjection tore the veil which the trembling fingers of her thoughts was weaving, and her face became rigid, her eyes faded, her voice a rough, unpleasant noise,

"Oh no, Guste, the boy just brings misfortune, trust me, husband, I know better." When she saw how the old man was listening tensely, she hesitated and tore herself away violently from a secret prohibition. She misled her husband and concluded,

"The woman doesn't confer it on us. Who lends to the second choice today and is still in business, hey?!"

The lies against the train of her soul made her deathly pale. Like someone who deprives themselves of hope by weakness and then in remorse is heavily depressed, she took a quick step back to the stool and sank down on it. Her legs immediately began to waggle again and she seized each knee so that it was at peace.

Then the great silence of helplessness lay on her body again; only the wispy, white hair quivered with the beat of her heart.

During this her husband berated her constantly, and although, numbed by her inner being, she did not understand a word, she felt his sorrow from the sound of his voice. This sense joined with her suffering and alienated it from her so that she rose to dispose of it through work.

She looked around for her stove cloth. It was hanging on a bucket in the corner next to the shelf of pots. Six dirty boards diagonally across to a crooked chair — a long way separated her from it.

Ill-tempered, she measured the distance with faded eyes, then she looked at the fire.

It had gone out a long time ago.

The chugging seething of the flame, the song of being home, was silent.

The evening wind had led the sun behind the mountains and was now caught sluggishly in the forest branches. Its great wings lay spread motionless across the darkening forests, where there was a glimmer, yet weaker like on the scales of dead fish. So even the song of the mountains was silent. The trees only stirred sometimes, soundless in the resting oscillation of the wind which no longer drove the dragging of dreamlike steps around the shelters of mankind.

The crack in the wall of time had closed again; softly, like the heart of the unborn, the pulse of the night was beating again.

All that took the tired will to work, the last defense against her fate, from the old woman's soul.

She took a strong, deep breath, set the crooked chair right, sat down and laid her upper body over the table so that her head came to rest on the right arm she had thrown over the brown table top.

But her face was turned towards the room and her faded eyes lay motionless, without sight. Old Wiesner in the adjoining room was constantly turning the basket between his legs again and grumbling about it.

From time to time he stooped further forward and looked at his wife. At these moments, he let out a growling cough to remind her of her work. When he had done this a few times in vain, he tentatively chewed a few curses and complaints between his toothless jaws so that his grey beard stirred thrusting.

Even that was no use, and so he finally blew the air through his nose angrily and reached for his sticks. But, even when he thereby clattered threateningly against the legs of his stool, his wife did not stir. This silent defiance, her mysterious words before, the entire constricting heaviness which lay in the room, it all put a fright into him so that he laid the sticks on the floor again and resumed turning the basket between his knees.

Hanne, however, lay motionless over the table. Her eyelids only twitched occasionally to cool the burning of her eyeballs, and her face became even paler.

In the world outside, the petering out was over and a golden brown shimmer was climbing up in waves.

It unfastened the bonds of her soul so that it was gliding down again into the circles of her greyed desire,

"Must hub and wheel be one ...? — What happens if the wheel spins out of its socket — — — not good — — if it has to spin out?" she asked fate to its changeless face.

Her husband, however, believed the words were directed at him and became furious,

"Dammit, dog damned dawdling, that! What would that be!? — A joke, a loud joke! That's what happens when you read with a lamp. — — Get up dear! The fire is out; make so that the beets fly into the bucket. — Hey, aren't you listening, the cows are restless already!"

Thus he shouted so that it sounded more like groaning. Then he hewed angrily at the basket. But in Hanne the flood of her innermost being restlessly climbed up further out of the hollows in which it had sobbed a lifetime; from the sand hills on which it had expired a thousand times; from the rocks which it had smashed against so often in vain.

"Everything is going downhill, the red light, the water, the leaves, the stones ... my life, my wheel, even that runs where everything is running to. — But, oh, how long my slope is, how gruesomely deep the hole where it finally tips over forever."

These words came monotonously from her mouth again, like the sounds with which a withered forest talks.

"Jokes, dammit!" Wiesner growled meanwhile; but his fear was growing.

He raised himself with the help of his sticks, so carefully that not the slightest noise was made, and appeared in the doorway.

His large, hulking shadow thrust itself across the floorboards like a threatening eclipse of the growing red embellishing the sparseness of the tiny room. With that Hanne was torn from her thoughts. She straightened up her upper body, laid her hands on her restive knees and stared at him as though he was an uncalled for intruder, with a quiet horror as though he was an enemy.

"Stop," she said softly to him, "I'm not afraid anymore. Fortune isn't walking about our house anymore, it doesn't need to anymore either. — Don't make one of those faces, sit down on the bench, sit down, sit down, sit down ..."

In dull fright, the old man listened and then looked tensely at his gaunt wife as if he could drive away with his steady, helpless gaze the silence which had already taken possession of her again.

"Brush your hair back," he said finally with unusual gentleness.

With an unbelieving, bitter smile at him, she pushed the frail, white wisps back and then turned her face to him,

"Was it never easy in your life as long as you were together with me?"

Wiesner lowered his head before her searching eyes, thrust his lower lip a little forward and thought for a while; after a long while, he just shook his head in great sadness.

"Were you never pleased about how the head forester lent us money when we were short, and that he provided for us and helped us. I was still pretty then."

In vain the old woman struggled against an agitation which was breaking her voice into quaking breaths.

"No, with regard to that, it was quite difficult at first," Wiesner answered, completely sunken in the memory of his work-heavy and yet so unsuccessful life.

"But weren't you happy about the gifts?"

"Happy! Such a master gives what he must, no more. He gifts nothing."

"Well and what did Wolf get from him then? And he was with him for thirteen years!"

"Truth is what's true. Truly yes, and it was no little thing, no, the envy had to be dropped, competently, industriously, managed, a heart-breaker even."

"You see, and he would have needed it to with his seven children, ha, all alive — all — all —"

"You're right, and all like watercress. — — Perhaps, if ours had not all died, perhaps it would have been different. So I always thought when I carried a little white coffin over the little hill again: one more angel for heaven, one mouth less at the table. That's what I consoled myself with! But perhaps it wasn't for the best. — Who knows?!"

A stone falls in a well. Then an indistinct, dull singing arises in the depths. Like a heavy bird, it climbs out of the night below us, the night over which we wander ignorantly; heavily laden with tales which have been sleeping silently below, it floats upward. Then we listen silently for a long time and swallow the expectation within us.

Thus the two old people both fell silent for a while in the workings of their life which the woman had torn open with her last strength.

"Oh, all, all, all," she spoke in dull lament to her hands. "If only Lisa had remained. She had beautiful locks, yellow as gold, and was only three weeks old when she died. — But we should-n't go there next to each other like two draught animals, between us the drawbar which tears the one over and the other under ... so they die, one after the other, all eight ... and every time fortune goes further away from the house and appears weaker ... but, they had to die, have I forgotten, they had to! There was no help from the pastor and none from a doctor."

"Now Hanne, they are dead now; but had to! — Weren't they all thick as noodles and fat? — I tell you: they died from our poverty alone."

"Not at all. Thick and fat! — They all just struggled so much, they all just screamed so loud; but they were without the most essential. And for that, you were at fault. You gave merely the body to each and I bore it into the world. But that by which a man lives, that was missing; for a child develops differently from a cow. — You! — You!! — But how could you fix that?! You were never good to me, never, never."

Fetching deep breaths, she stopped, but straightaway engaged passionately again when she saw how her husband was getting ready to speak. He could only bring forth an initial grumble. She cut it off firmly,

"At first I didn't know; but, when the fourth had died, then I knew it. It lay in its eyes. Oh, and they all had it, that sniffling, the blank in a dog's eyes, Jesus, the entire sordidness — — — and if it had gone away, the blackness in which every woman is immersed in her heavy hours, and I was shown my child and its eyes sparkled, then I would have been able to strike against the wall if I had been strong enough. The strength always came back afterwards, but a fury remains over the child, which I never get out of my heart, with nothing, not with prayers, not with thinking. — — Thus I poisoned them, all of them, from the first to the last. — Only the boy remained, for I had to be tormented so that I could atone for them all."

Wiesner did not hear the last sentence in his horror, but cried out from his self-absorption,

"You poisoned them, you! — That just can't be, you're crazy!"

"As I said, not a hair otherwise, I'm not crazy. Every one, I poisoned every one, I poisoned them with my breast-milk. It ate away at their hearts," she answered firmly.

"Crazy! Old woman! Haha! I'll be damned! Dammit, with the milk, yours! Poison?"

He made violent endeavours to return to his old gruffness.

Hanne insisted doggedly.

"Laugh for my sake, if you can. From what does a child develop, from what does it live? From love. — Ha and don't I have to poison them with my fury, with my sorrow — don't I have to? You, husband, what do you say now?"

Every feature of her face was sharpened, her eyes stared fearfully as, with this question, she straightened up with effort.

The old man wanted to continue laughing. But when he half-turned his head to look at her with forced superiority, his laughter turned into fright. Touching his beard stunned, he stuttered something and broke off with a high sound.

His wife started abruptly and stared fixedly down in front of herself,

"I had to ... silence, silence ... I had to ... for only thus could I live ... I had — to ..." she murmured exhaling.

"Then you would have, as you say, have killed them all?" Wiesner began after a long silence.

In his voice lay the awkward caution of a hard hand travelling over a wound.

Hanne slowly raised and lowered her head and stammered desperately,

"All of them, Ronnie, Franz, Kath, Lisa — — all of them, all of them, until my desire had tired! Then the children finally stopped. Now I am like a withered leaf. I have given everything and gotten nothing for it. A thousand nights I've trembled, a thousand days I've waited. — You! — Am I right, your feet walk on over hearts?"

She stammered thus and for a long time kept raising and lowering her head as if her words had been corrupted by the convulsions of her feverish lips. Sweat appeared on the forehead of the one-eyed man.

"I'm hot," he said.

Hanne did not stir.

"The cherry tree is turning yellow," he began again, "marigolds are growing by the barn wall. It looks like the evening is coming too. It hasn't been so red for a long time."

His wife quickly raised her head and asked fearfully,

"Where is it coming?"

"Now, there, look, Hanne!"

Wiesner lifted his arm pointing. Only it was shaking so much that he immediately let it fall again out of shame.

Hanne stared wide-eyed into the glow which was flowing into the tree in full stream so that the leaves stirred softly under the shimmering burden.

"How deftly it's done," she said, cherishing the view completely, "as if everything was blooming, everything was singing. It's still growing. When is there an end? and — a day perishes. Oh, but how a person dies, how awfully, for no life is beautiful."

She had coined her last breath into words as if not to destroy the trembling brilliance gliding over her soul. Now she was exhaustedly tearing new air into her breast.

"Yes, yes; it all goes away. That won't change. I am seventy, why am I still waiting! Eight ropes are pulling me, for every dead child is probably like a tether which binds me to the grave."

The death song of her words filled the entire room, and Wiesner passed his hand over his eyes a few times, for he thought that the grey haze which seemed to come from every object arose from the weakness of his sight.

"Whoever invented age should be struck dead with a mace. No strength in the legs, short of breath, no teeth in the mouth."

His wife looked at him indifferently. She felt how he wanted to steal past again and her face puckered as if she was smiling contemptuously.

The shame of seeing himself recognised drove him to defiance of the ruthless one. He clothed his trepidation in a reproach against her,

"Hm, what you wanted all evening. You have bent your back ineffectually, I have interrupted myself. It doesn't go any different."

Hanne straightened up gravely,

"Point the finger there finally, there, to where I have perished! — Working! That is the breath which my father and mother gave to me. I have never wanted to sleep on the hay in the sun. But I never had two eyes for nothing. See, the one belongs to the body, the other to the soul. With the one I see into your room, with the other I can see above myself. And because we should be quiet sometimes and stretch out, for that reason alone probably does God have the stars, the sun and the tree keeping watch over us, the birds and the beautiful clouds. The left eye is the one that looks up, the one that stands over the heart. But you must never have had one. Then God himself hewed out your left eye with a cane, because it was unneeded. — Oh, how the senseless cattle are better than many men. You, look at the wagtail, how many thousands of times it runs up and down the furrows. But in the end it shoots up in the air and makes its cheerful song. But ... hahaha!"

Shrilly, she broke out with piercing laughter because it was all there. She entwined her hands and bowed her head so low that the wisps on her temples, loosening themselves more than usual, ran together in front of her face like a trembling veil.

The old man's throat constricted. He arduously hauled his crooked body upright by the table and grasped onto it.

"Hanne ..." He did not bring produce anything more.

His old wife unclasped her hands and stroked her hair into her headscarf. Only a little strand slipped away from her grasp and hung over her eyes. She reached for it with her crooked, clumsy fingers until she had gathered it, rubbed the wispy hair between her index finger and thumb and spoke her defence to it,

"I know, I know; you well know, you have heard a thousand times with your roots what is haunting the inside of my head the past few years, I want nothing more, just peace, peace before the end."

"Hanne ..." the waiting old man asked more urgently.

"Husband."

With gentle voice, she finally indicated that she was listening to him, and turned her head to him as, close to falling over, he held onto the table with his last strength.

"Sit down first!" her clemency demanded when she saw him suffering so.

"Husband," she then began just as gently, "why haven't you taken my hand even once in our forty five years and called to me like now. — Perhaps, slow-moving, like one of those quite thin strands, we have found each other. You would not have tortured yourself through each day ill-temperedly, you would not have struck me, what was in me, what is dead now, would have come over you, perhaps more beautifully like the redness which lies there between the trees outside now ... oh, and then all the children would have remained alive and everything ... even the other ..."

In agonising disappointment, she felt her features slackening with her words and heard her murmur becoming ever more indistinct with the bitterness of a man who hears ever softer the steps of departing friends who wanted to rescue him from his great need and are now creeping away cowardly at a favourable moment.

But his wife's hidden torment was appearing to Wiesner now too. He had, his face buried in both hands, listened in silence. Now he raised his head and snuffled.

"Hanne, how far are we two from the grave? Come, let us walk the last stretch together."

After a long struggle, she answered with the greatest effort,

"The boy is there …"

"Now, that is okay."

She moved her head in disagreement.

"If the woman from Wartha lends the money then Guste will take over the business and we will go into retirement," he insisted to her.

The old woman remained in a dismissive silence; her grief was becoming visible, and she had to turn her face away.

"I won't talk you into it!" he began again consolingly. "He is marrying; a handsome man, upright, like a man of law, he is even getting one with money. Afterwards we can creep into the room and if God wills it you can still cradle children who haven't died there."

Hanne sprang up with signs of great fright and looked at him with such a disturbed face that he broke off confused.

After some deliberation, he said ill-temperedly to himself,

"Now, why couldn't that be everything?!"

With these words from the man, a part of the evening glow died away, like flames lapsing under collapsed embers, and half the room sank into semidarkness. It happened so abruptly that Hanne started and looked around as if something had slid from her with the vanishing light. Then she stepped, as if to repeat it, with solemn strolling stride from the shadows into the fullness of the evening light still flowing strongly and fully in through the little window by the door, and she looked praying with wide-eyes into God's flood.

As she thus gazed and let herself be blessed, a tremor went through her withered body once more; but it became slowly weaker, and the light had made her quite strong in the end. Then she took herself back to her place. Her step had the wavering of ripe grain swaying against the blade of the cutter. She stepped thus to her seat and looked once more at her husband who followed it all incomprehensibly with helpless eyes.

Hesitantly she then let herself down and lapsed against her will into a musing with open eyes.

Meanwhile the evening light was becoming milder. It migrated falteringly floorboard by floorboard further from the door. The exultation of its dying, still seething red like death in the falling leaves of wild vines, took on the soft glow which sleep brings to the cheeks of children. It thus stood now between the doorposts and prepared with flickering tremors to take leave.

When Hanne perceived this change in the light, she was startled like a wanderer who stops too long for a rest just before his goal and now rises in great haste to complete with hurried steps the small remainder of his journey.

"The boy," she thus began, "the boy ... ... that's just why nothing works anymore. If you had had a heart then you would have had an eye for all our misery, and my shame wouldn't have become so old."

Then she waited with rapt breath for her husband's response.

The world of his soul had finally passed before his eyes, and he stared frightened into the expanse of this terribleness. The habitual life of his handiwork was extinguished, and he noticed that he had lived quite differently from how he had wanted. A soft dim light had flowed from his wife's words across the path which he had strolled against his will.

"Did you know everything then, about the path?" he asked and let his glance glide over the inconceivability of this inner confusion.

"I knew everything; but I could not stop it."

"Oh no, no! Known, well yes yes, right, like to-morrow is a day too?"

"No, like I have five fingers on my hand and two eyes in my head, I knew like that."

"Well, if so and it had all gone on. Then you could have given the cart a shove on the other side."

"I did, God in heaven is my witness, I just wanted our happiness with it. What someone can try, I have done.

We were just two years married. You pushed and cursed me and boozed about, we argued from the first day onward. The bruises did not go away from one day to the next. I consumed myself with work. And what we earned did not remain; we saved and had nothing.

Then I thought in my fear of heaven, perhaps, if you can live better, you will see me and we will find each other, and there would be a heaven over our house. The way it *once* had been in my head hasn't gone away from me: it goes where I go, works with me, where I sleep it speaks, and when I drive it away, it becomes worse. In the end, I don't know anymore where my heart beats. Like a glittering merry-go-round, it turns me. Then it happened. And as he promised it, so it was. We could buy the business, he gave us the seed, the wood; he made the heavy fields ..."

The woman fell silent from exhaustion. She then looked timidly to her husband, who, both elbows propped up, stared at the table with his deeply bowed head; no breath stirred his self-absorption.

And because she thought that he was now blind as well, she brought herself together for the last bitter step and said with gentle voice, dropping off after each word,

"Then ... came ... his ... boy ..."

"That didn't need to be said," he murmured, recovering arduously from the blow, encumbered however with no movement of his stony self-absorption.

Then he gnashed against the tabletop,

"So the head forester ... such an accursed hound ... the devil has fetched him ... the boy? ... the *boy*? ... haha ... and I am still proud of it ... ape, ape, ape! I, I, I ... — Oho! that's why! ... Now, why didn't you poison him! like the others?"

The question remained without an answer; it lost itself in the room which seemed filled with a seething air like a disturbed fly coming to rest in the night.

Hanne had crept out and was going up the stairs.

Wiesner knew nothing of it all. He had even forgotten his own question already and was listening as it flowed down humming past his ears.

The world of his soul was black.

Night lay on its turbid terribleness.

With pounding heart, he asked for light,

"... Hanne! ... Hanne!! ... Am I a hound? — are you a hussy? — Oh no! ... I just acted as if I knew nothing; but I probably felt it every time when you kissed me on the forehead ... and everything you bore ... not an angry word ... always good — — — no, it doesn't make you a hussy ... Hanne!!"

He finally cried out thus in torment.

"Here I am," the answer came from the door. The voice sounded weak and gentle, the way children speak who have run themselves out of breath.

The sound seemed so odd to Wiesner that he was a little startled and looked at Hanne's chair. When he found it empty, he waited awhile to collect himself, then he said timidly,

"I can't see you."

"Here," she spoke just as softly.

Deep darkness was already filling the room. In the house, only a shimmer of pale light still lay as it finally decamped from the valleys to stroll towards the vanishing twilight. It also staggered and smouldered, lending everything sharp contours for one last time.

In this pale light, Wiesner saw his wife standing. She was adorned as though going to church. The red roses on her crumpled straw hat moved swaying over her forehead as she nodded to him and, at the same time, drew the black scarf tighter around her shoulders.

Wiesner knew everything and asked stiffly with an unnaturally soft voice,

"Then do you really want to go now?"

She moved her head in affirmation so that the red roses swayed, and she remained silent.

"You have no shoes," the old man began again and pointed at her naked feet.

"I have none, not for years anymore. God will not resent me it if I come to him barefoot," the old woman answered in humble faith.

Wiesner became hot with the tone in her voice. He grasped distractedly at the table edge and struggled against the choking in his chest.

"You're talking in a high voice like a child," he asked with his last strength.

For a long time, Hanne just swung the roses of her hat as answer, and her face became blissful at the same time.

Finally she answered,

"I have peace now too. Everything is extinguished. I don't know why; I feel like a child."

"Are you angry with me?" the old man asked, a numbness having come over him.

"Oh my God, whoever has to go, carries others in their heart."

Then she turned to the door.

"Hanne, must you really; can't it work anymore otherwise?" Wiesner asked with trembling mouth.

She appeared in the door once more and looked one last time into the room.

"I must," she then said mutely.

"Where should I look for you, Hanne?"

"Where Dittert Klemens lay."

"In the quarry?!"

Suddenly the old woman's entire body began to tremble, her jaws clattered against each other, heavy moans struggled from her heaving chest, and she had to lean against the doorpost.

"You," Wiesner asked with a voice made hard by the desperate struggle against sobbing.

The unsparing sound of this word called the entire torment of their marriage to consciousness and dispelled the last fit of life from her body.

"No," she breathed and straightened up, "the last red is creeping into the forest. Adieu! I won't find the way otherwise."

With that she disappeared.

At the corner by the door she banged against the wooden bench. The tin cans on it clanged angrily against each other. Then the shuffling that naked feet make when they skim scuffing the ground with hurried steps could be heard a few more times, becoming ever softer. Then even this last sign of his wife's life was extinguished in the deep gloaming, and it seemed to him as if every thing was gliding like a heavy, black shadow into it, never to be seen again, numb, turbid, formless.

With gentle fingers, the night burrowed into the tree which rustled shivering in its first sleep. The idle jarring of corn crakes ran through the grass. The crickets fell silent and then sang again for themselves. The running stream counted its waves aloud.

Suddenly there is a crack somewhere in the room, as though someone has crept in soundlessly and is now bumping about since they want to sit down in the darkness.

Wiesner is startled, holds his breath and listens.

It is nothing. The night speaks its old sounds again.

Then yearning and remorse seizes him like a temper. Strength comes to him abruptly and he does not know that he is lame, springs up and screams despairingly,

"Hanne, wait, I'm going with you!"

In the middle of the room, he bangs with his head into the bench by the oven so that blood immediately streams over his hand from the deep wound.

He attempts to get up a few more times.

In vain.

The blood keeps flowing.

The darkness becomes thicker; a flickering streaming comes into the night around him. His eyes are closed and he does not stir anymore so as not to disturb his ears from following his fleeing wife with his hearing.

All the sounds in the distance become manifest to him: the forest gently sings its deep song — the blackbird's call peters out lullingly — a roebuck roars — and then, muffled by the distance, a shrill scream falls through the air.

Horrified, Wiesner tears his head up. He supports his upper body on both hands and stares at the forest over which a light stands like the fixed shimmer of broken eyeballs.

"That was no goshawk and no barn owl," he sagged. "Now she is there."

Then he sank down from weakness.

The Last Child

A gift to my wife:

Take this song! It has in a period of anger
Freed me from earth's greatest torture.
And if it releases you too from old hurt,
Then it is doubly dear to my heart.

H eaven is the soul of the earth. In it the bells of life and death sound ceaselessly. And on every strike of the eternal hour, an angel disengages from the wide expanses and floats down to the world of the earth.

The bell of death sounds differently, hard and stormy, or as the soft song of a bird sounds; the rope of necessity is pulled depending on the rattle of an old heart or the last wavering of a young breast.

S pring is strolling over the mountains so that the forests are usurping the blue of heaven; little bells trip through the valleys and follow behind silvery brooks running on the soles of their winged feet, and young green life swells from the hearts of the trees.

When it stepped through the lanes of the towns and villages, the young people raised a hue and cry, the men grasped tighter in their work; but the old people and the pregnant women felt their end. They hauled themselves into their beds, their bodies became wilted, their eyes sought in the expanses for help, tormented breaths welled from their mouths, and with trembling hearts, they chimed the bells of necessity so that God took pity on the conflicted nature of their life and rescued them to the joy of hours or of eternity.

Thus the sound of bells toned confusedly in heaven, its gates standing wide open. For the angels of death and life floated in long trains in and out, and the double-doors to the eternal hall could never shut.

Two angels of death sank down to earth on their wings one night in this very spring. When they arrived where the circle of stars stopped and the restless streams of the earth were interwoven, the leading, pale spirit turned his face back and paused a little until his comrade had caught up to him with heavy wingbeats.

"Now our ways part", he said to him.

"Oh no, I must also go down into the realm of men who dig the fire out of the earth", the nearing angel responded with humbly bowed forehead, and in his voice rang the shrill tone of terrestrial pain. Then the white cloud of their heavenly beauty streamed into further depth; the first spirit more garishly, like the leaf of a lily, the second still cumbered by the outlines of a human body swimming like a shadow in its glory.

The first glided without a sound, like the snow sinking through still air, but the second stimulated the air around himself, and the nearer they came to earth, the more audibly the breath, the grief-stricken song of humanity, rang from the midst of his being.

The mountains of earth emerged just then under them like black islands.

"Let us wait on this peak a little. The soul which I shall be given to lead to heaven is strengthening itself in its last slumber for its last walk. But the torment of the earth is affecting me", the tired angel said.

They folded their wings and sat down. The power of the earth tore the shadow-heavy one to a rough plunge. But the purified one caught him compassionately and cushioned his white head kindheartedly on his chest.

"You are too stormy, brother", he whispered at the same time. "You should not still have to expect such weight."

A trembling ran through the cushioned spirit and he remained silent for a long time. Finally he raised his face and asked,

"Isn't anguish a meal which doubles itself when you eat slowly?"

The strong angel looked down into the sad eyes which had been raised up to him question-ingly; but although he noticed how a tremor stirred them, he did not hold back with the reproach of his love and said,

"Only if such a courage tortures itself, how will you exist in the difficult hours, how will you help it and everyone, when you are already so troubled in yourself? You should have asked the eternal goodness before."

Then the trembling came over the tarrying angel even stronger, and his eternal soul became so full of helplessness that he looked straight in front of himself and watched with an empty glance as the wind gently covered and exposed the clouds over the firs on the mountain, like a child dressing and undressing its dolls. At the same time, the stream of air hummed a monotonous song, and the trees stirred their branches in sleep.

"I know. I know", the sorrowful angel then began with lowered voice, "Oh, my poor mother who only bore for death!"

A long silence followed the words of deep sadness again.

And the wind moved away, the mist stopped billowing and spread itself out evenly like a becalmed sea. The sleep of the trees became black and inflexible, all things melted away as though into an immobile sullenness. Only the two angels blossomed in the night of the earth like two bright white flowers, and shimmering threads ran out from them on all sides. Suddenly, the afflicted spirit raised his right arm, stretched it out away from himself and drew it through the resting mist.

It stirred with it.

With a bitter smile, he remarked on it.

"Do you see all that?" he turned to his companion and pointed with his eyes to his arm.

There the contours of a human arm had emerged more ruggedly and blacker in the shimmeringly beautiful form of his body.

"How this cleavage must torture you!" the other angel answered him compassionately.

"Now, you see, and if I also lead countless souls out of hardship to him, it won't let go of me. It is beautiful that unfulfilled desire thrusts through the clouds and the feet of love also stride over our grave, but motherly love robs me of heavenly peace.

You know, my mother is half shadow. With every child that she bears to the grave, she becomes stranger on earth. Her best and deepest parts die with her little dead ones on the other side. Thus her body goes to ruin like a neglected house.

Mostly she walks drunk on the dreams passing through her head. From time to time, however, her terrestrial eyes become seeing and recognise her misery. Then she clings onto her husband. And her fruit, fathered in fear, carried in fright and born in shock, is homeless on earth from the first day of its life. The blue walls of the gaunt little body does not hold for long the soul which augments the strength for flight with every breath. Soon the little heart gives up its struggle exhausted, and often only days after the birth, staring from the cradle in the little room of my parents are two deadened infant's eyes again."

The brasher spirit let his brother, still wandering thus in the shadow of earthly difficulty, talk. For he knew that laments were the best cure for sorrow, and when he now finished, he looked at the grieved one consolingly.

But he was completely under the spell of his body and continued, "Yet I fell from the lap of my mother harder into the drudgery of life. My soul probably also shook for the eternal freedom past the stars, but my heart continually tore me from the fists of illness, and at three years old, I seemed to my parents to be saved. They went around like they were redeemed and ate their hard bread laughing.

In my fifth summer, I too fell. The fever tore me from the lane and tortured the soul from my body in one night. Since then the spirit of my mother wanders around God's gate and, crying, demands me back to life, and her desire won't let the love of blood in me and the dead body with her to be completely extinguished. The other thousands of billions stand in exultation before Jehovah, while the singing to the Blessed Jesus falls from my mouth like a wilted flower.

A few times, it seemed as if she would yet be able to forget me because a child had climbed from her body again. Yet my hope that time might be able to liberate me was an illusion. My little brother already lay dying again, and my mother called to me for help, me, the angel of death. Now I hurry driven by eternal command and the love for my blood. The one power that I can't escape, and don't want to, ordered the life of my brother, before the morning prevailed, to be annihilated, the other begged fearfully to me to spare it.

And if human sympathy overwhelms me down there before its torment, then I am lost to heaven and for the return to the world alike and must wander homeless as a spirit of the air for ever between heaven and earth."

Thus spoke the angel of death. His voice was becoming more and more earth-weary, and his illness came over him deeper. The impure shadow of his life was climbing from the earth, a life which they embedded in the grave in vain, and it superimposed itself more and more clearly on his glory so that the transfiguration only lay around him like a tremulous husk.

At the same moment, two poor people rose up out of the haze of the deep, gaunt and taut like stretched ropes, and withered hands full of anguish grasped seeking for the body which lay in its pale glory as though in a protective case.

At the same time, a cry of pain rang out weakly from the earth,

"Why are you dead to me? Come at least and stand by me."

Then the anguish-troubled angel sprang from the lap of the other and tried to flee. But he only made a few awkward steps, like a heavy bird that wants to fly up, then he was torn from the burden of his shadow-body to earth. At the same time, his soul groaned in such fear that the trees were startled from their sleep and the wind thrown from their crowns, gliding down, stretching out half-asleep and then creeping back again into its pleasant nest, circuitously and snarling like the drowsy lying themselves down to sleep.

The purified spirit swayed to him, slung his arm in shock around the fallen one and raised him up. His eternal light drove the shadow out of his brother's glory so that the human body only lay in it like an impure breath.

"My brother!" the re-straightened one stammered in overflowing thanks. The spirits lay breast to breast, and their souls chimed in each other like the tones of pure harps.

Then the glory of the Lord smouldered as a golden cloud in the distance, and the air began to tremble more and more.

"Oh Trinity!" With this cry, the tested angel threw himself towards the eternal light. "Don't let me fall into torment, and if you will then I will lead my mother's heart into your peace too."

But before his cry had faded, the shimmer of the eternal one dived down again into endlessness, and the air stood like a faltering breath in the night. Distressed, the angels of death returned to their place, for they did not know whether the Lord had strolled past to console or as a serious warning.

Whilst they were still talking about it, a gentle tone, like the call of a naked bird desiring its way out of the egg with powerless little beak, sank to them from the heights.

"Did you hear that?" the beset spirit asked and touched the hand of the other.

The latter just nodded in affirmation. With that the locks of his parting fell over his face so that the air of his compassion could not be seen in it; his eyes just stood behind the shimmering veil like two specks of rain-sated blue sky.

"My hour has come!" the shadow-sick angel spoke and rose, for the call of necessity floated past them again. Then he stood a while before the assured angel, who had also risen and, after a short pondering of the sorrow, held him in his arms full of ardency.

When the spirits had imbued each other with love, they spread their wings and sank down to earth.

The shores of earth were rising ever sharper out of the darkness of night, and the first sounds were becoming audible: the shrill whistle of an iron wagon, the hollow roar of piped steam and the grumbling moans that is given out by the lightning which drives men. Soon the angels of death also perceived the first chimneys from whose heights the stinking smoke sank over the rooves of the village. After midnight the black flues stood thick as a forest of trees stripped of their branches.

The beauty of the assured spirit glided thither. But towards morning, where an avenue of vast lime trees stretched from the nearby mountains to the village as if the trees were marching to safeguard the afflicted humanity, the smaller cottages were already appearing and the blessing of the ploughshare was sleeping in the silent lanes. The now quite solitary angel of death skimmed for a moment over the entwined tree-tops of the avenue and directed his eyes fearfully to his companion. He saw him float like a milk-white veil before the golden glow of distant coke ovens and vanish in an abrupt fall.

Then he too became invisible and let himself down through the branches to the road.

After a short stroll, he turned onto a short, narrow path which was hemmed in on both sides by an old wooden fence. The crooked gate of slats, which was meant to shut the path off from the road, had sunk with its latch from the crude hooks which thrust into the aged lime tree, and it was hanging there broken. A grey speck stood out from the trunk of the lime tree at head-height.

The young leaves of the old tree absorbed the light of the distant, hazy moon and let it glide down, laden with the full scent of its beauty, so that a softly glimmering veil lay around about.

This and the dull smell which filled the narrow path brought forth a gentle feeling of home in the angel of death. Before he had become truly aware of this, he opened the rotten little gate which creaked with its rusted hinges.

At this sound, fumbling steps were heard in the little house to which the path led and which lay in the shadow of the windowless back walls of two hulking houses. The front door opened, and while the hesitant hand of the person stepping out slowly closed it again, the lamenting sound of a woman's voice rang out from within. The clicking of the lock cut it off.

"Who is there! — What could it be! — There must be someone there!" a man's voice asked with uncertain gruffness into the silence of the dull path.

It was Garbe, the tailor, the mortal father of the angel. He waited awhile for an answer; then he came down the path and found under the lime tree in the trembling white darkness of the night that the gate to the garden was open. He shook his head in worried astonishment, pressed the latch into the crude hooks and murmured,

"It just pushes itself today. I should be concerned. — It was opened, I heard it go quite well from within and nobody is here, no wind stirs ..."

Then he propped himself on the crossbar of the gate with his elbows and stared into the night.

"Just nothing remains for us", he spoke dully to himself. "Nothing is any use; I just have to see that I keep my head. — But ... but ... why in all the world must such a little thing suffer so much! Doesn't it know to make an end with a yelp!"

His dead child, the angel of death, stood invisibly behind him as he spoke thus, and directed the eyes of his being grasping at him.

Garbe felt an inner frisson from it, but thought his soul was being beset by a weakness and straightened up,

"No, no! I will survive this time too. Without a doubt", with that he lifted his fist and threatened wildly into the night, "I'm defending myself already ... the damned crying, I'll finish everything, will make an end once more!"

"Go and raise mother, she is lying before the cradle!" his child whispered into his soul.

The sweat of fear appeared on the forehead of the tailor, he groaned and stroked his hand over his face,

"Oh her! It suffocates me so, it is the absolute worst of all!" he answered to the hidden being which spoke behind him to his inner being. "Old trousers, torn jackets, rags, always just rags! And when my wife is finished and must be gone! I must not think of that at all."

Always in the fear of this greater misfortune than the certain death of his little boy lying inside in a spasmodic slumber, he turned from the little gate and struck out with the fragments of his thoughts as though with straying hands at this blackness.

His going was a backing away, for he had the feeling that a power was following him which nothing could reconcile. This inner darkness lay before his eyes, and although it was so light that the contours of every object were recognisable, if also blurred, he had to feel his way along the wooden fence until he came to where the tottery fence had made an outward spring and widened the narrow path into a small, just as dull court-yard.

Suddenly the suspicion came to the tailor that someone had stolen his wood, and he straight-away sat down by the pile of old mine timber and began to count, feeling with both hands the fronts of the round pieces of wood. He sought the thick stave, and it seemed to him that his situation was hopeless, frightful, if this solid, hale piece had been stolen. But he did not find it and continued counting, kneeling, his arms outspread with trembling hands; at the same time, he murmured disjointed words of hope and lament, of pain and fury at the large, beautiful piece of wood.

His dead child stood shaking in merciful love at his left side. The stream of life which leads to the Father of everything, and which we call being dead, held him away from him.

Garbe suddenly let both his arms fall soundlessly.

After a while of hanging his head dully, he stooped to his left to give room for one last hope by seeking for the heavy piece of wood in the gap between the woodpile and the rabbit hutch. With that he came too close to the circle of death next to him, and he saw into the world which lies behind all things. There stood his recently deceased child, close enough to touch and yet irretrievably out of reach.

In extreme fright, the tailor shot up, stared at the dull path smouldering with light, stuttered the name of his child and his entire body shook.

But the wall of his senses had already shut again and the fear increased before something incomprehensible which tortured his entire soul and before a power which he drew further back from into the little courtyard and which he tried to shake off from himself,

"It has just that and such on earth which is strange! ... no, no ... I can't defend myself enough ... no, no ... and she is in misery, she has just a lousy way", he murmured.

There is a sickness which consists of a man having the agonising feeling of losing his guts. With this feeling in emotional respects, everything sinks, everything sinks out of him for which he has suffered and waited, for which he took on scorn and hunger, his entire soul, so that he is as though extinguished and only has the consciousness of looking at this torment. This feeling was very strong in him. In the helplessness of his poor spirit, he found no other means against this self-dissolution than rescuing himself with the belief in his undiminished possessions.

He stooped down to the rabbit hutch before which he was standing, felt the crannies of the cover and pulled testing on the small padlock. Then he knelt down to see through the mesh-protected vent on the front wall into the inside of the rabbit hutch.

"Hansie! — Hans, Hans, Hans! — wss! — wswsws!" he whispered affectionately and stared with extreme attentiveness through the grill.

No sound stirred within.

"The old one usually stretches his nose out when I call just once", he said distrustfully and shook his head.

He plucked a handful of grass from next to the hutch and held it before the mesh with the insistent demand,

"Hansie, old boy! It's me, Hansie!"

Nothing stirred, not once did the shy buck kick out with its hind legs.

... He had not found the piece of wood, the hutch was empty, everything gone, everything ... the sweat rose on the tailor's forehead, and in extreme fear, he threw himself to the ground, brought his mouth close to the vent and enticed again and again with trembling voice,

"Hansie! wsws! — Hansie, Hans ... wswsws!"

And he still affected to call to the little pile of his possessions, and prayed ardently for the life of his wife and for his life, until he gave up the deception, propped his elbows up on the ground and stared into the night of his fate with eyes which saw nothing and a soul which prayed dully, bitterly, sobbing, full of discord, abject; but he kept whispering the same thing,

"... wsws ... wswsws ... wsss ... wss ... wswswsws ..."

In the end, it was just a hot breathing into the dew-cold grass, and his chest was pushing against the unfeeling earth.

"You must not die yet; your life has still not run out", the angel of death reminded his father.

Then the tailor stopped his whispering, sat up, struck his fist against his chest and said with fretful voice,

"Say what I don't know! — I know that myself. Say if you know it or not!"

For he thought his soul had spoken to him, and he was discontented with it because it spoke aloud in him so stupidly, and he maltreated himself with blows to bring his numbed soul to clear reflection.

"I know it all myself", he then spoke more calmly to himself and looked down the short path searchingly. "That I already know — and each thing has its necessity, its cause — yes — just so! And if everything will be, why in all God's world do I not have seven hard, shiny talers in my top cupboard? — Money is living and wants to live and to never die ... it is living, for it is from my blood ..."

The angel of death noticed with horror how the increasing compassion made his dead body stronger over him, and he straightened up in his sacred desire. Then the waves of his being came back to God again like cheerful fountains, and what his terrestrial compassion had hidden from him, he recognised clearly in the rays of his sleepless eyes again: he must not yet touch his father, for his soul was neither the leaf ready to fall, nor the bird waiting for its last song, but the heap of ants made fiercer by earthly happiness and running confusedly in the shadow of death passing by.

"Shoulder your destiny!" the angel of death intruded on him once more. "And when mother is embraced too, then a fear will fall from you and return as peace."

Garbe lifted his head and stared at the wisdom of death. But then the gates of his soul were too narrow, could not accept the wisdom and left it standing as an abyss before him. With dull eyes, the tailor looked into it.

Then the angel of the last hour knew that his father's life would have no end but would just start again.

For that reason, he turned to the house whose door had just been opened. He floated past the person stepping out and vanished within.

It was a large, hulking human body which had shoved itself through the doorway and, after a few deep breaths, now coughed.

"Garbe!" it called then with controlled urgency and repeated after a few looks with gentle pity, "Albin!"

The tailor knew who it was, and knew the reason why he was being called into the house; but, just for that reason, he remained seated on the ground before the rabbit hutch and did not answer, so as to also give a fright to that person by the silence which oppressed him and at the same time to avert the misfortune which she reported back in the house. But when he heard how her feet got ready to walk onto the crunching sand, he raised himself from the ground with the help of his hands and crept on tiptoes towards the massive shadow.

Before he suspected it, he bumped into her.

"Is that you? — Garbe! — Albin!" the voice called fearfully.

"Well yes, of course. Who else would it be, grandpa?" he answered grumpily.

"What are you doing outside? — Where were you?" she asked further.

But Garbe remained silent to hinder her from saying what he was afraid of.

But it was no help to him.

"The moon is low", she began anew. "The morning is coming — it's the time — you know it from the others — it pushes on just like them all — and towards the end, you know, after that it goes extremely fast — and she can't remain alone — I never know — she is so very down."

"You have a lot of flesh on you", Garbe replied in dull reproach. "— Mrs Gebeln — look."

He spoke these last words with gleeful schadenfreude that he was offending her so deeply.

"Why do you say Mrs Gebeln?"

"Because everyone is one and two. You are, it seems to me, just one. You see, but of me, there I know exactly that I am Albin Garbe and one more. The other, Jesus, what should I say to you! You, I am to you next to him like a boy and run around his legs ..."

Suddenly his words came in a rush.

"... when the doors move and nobody touches them; when what is there isn't there; when you talk and don't understand and know it and don't comprehend — then you leap over yourself and stand behind yourself and talk over your shoulders into your ears ..." Exhausted, he broke off.

"*Garbe! — Garbe!*" Mrs Gebeln cried in shock and shook him so that he would come to his senses. "If you had gotten neatly drunk; but so!"

But the tailor stood completely in thrall to the incomprehensible events, stepped closer to his grandmother, held her hand next to his mouth and whispered appealing,

"Let it well be, I don't know! Here he stood ..."

"Who?"

"I saw my one just now in heaven next to another angel."

"Ah you mean ..."

"Now just like him" — he did not give the name out of fear — "he stood here where you stand right now, as if he was in body and living, graspable ..."

"Stop!"

"... don't have to, don't have to ... when the dead walk around and are ..."

"You!" —

Mrs Gebeln pointed with urgent seriousness to the house from which long, pining sounds were coming. The tailor, talkative out of need, suddenly turned silent and lowered his face stubbornly.

"Come, Albin, we have to be with her. It is happening. Albin, you!" she called weakly, since Garbe did not stir. Suddenly he broke up and struck himself as though distressed.

"I can't! I can't this time! You can probably do with me what you want!"

These words were screamed in the way that an exhausted game animal turns on its hunter when it sees him raising his hand for the last blow.

Mrs Gebeln did not bother herself with his despair, but took him by the arm and drew him to the door. The poor man leant back, shook his head towards the ground and murmured constantly between his teeth,

"But really, having to be there does nothing — it could n... it could n..."

"Now what then, for heaven's sake, only? Talk properly when you speak. With you two, I can't understand a thing!"

The grandmother said it with arduous control of her impatience, for she was ill-tempered from watchfulness. But soon she thought again of the misery of these two poor people and hence asked the bowed man once more in sparing love,

"What then, Garbe?"

The tailor answered with poignant voice,

"That she must die with it; right, isn't it?!"

"Oh that. Tine is more tenacious than I."

"Well, I'm just thinking too; I become so weak sometimes when it comes to a great handful of things about one."

She climbed the steps to the front door quicker, stepped on tiptoe through the narrow vestibule and then stopped and listened in silent assent at the living room door. Just then a thin, high woman's voice had raised itself, talking unintelligible words in festive singing tones.

"It is high time I went inside", Mrs Gebeln whispered.

"Yes, yes; she is already talking fine", Garbe finished and regretted not having stayed in the courtyard. The grandmother opened the door and stepped back to let Garbe in first.

The tailor hesitated a while and looked inquiringly into the room, because he had resolved in his anguish to flee if the misfortune had already progressed too far.

But everything was as always, and he entered without noticing that Mrs Gebeln had drawn back, closed the door from outside and gone away.

The ticking of the clock captured Garbe. It sounded peacefully and steadily through the dimness, through the heavy soul oppressed by struggle like seething hot air, and the little lamp on the table also still bore patiently the red little clump of light like before. The glass panes of the yellow-painted pot cupboard on the left wall were shimmering softly. The corners lay in darkness. Even with his cutting table by the rightmost of the two windows in the back wall, he saw nothing but the bright edge of the smoothly planed bench seat.

The morning hung before the window like a dirty pale sheet.

In the middle of the room, where he did not direct his eyes and most distinctly did not look, the cradle stood with his dying child still sleeping and only emitting from time to time a rattling sound like the banging of pots when a heavy gait goes across the floor. Then the tiny little hands would rise up confusedly every time and flounder in the air so that it looked as if grey moths were flying deathly drunk around the expiring little head.

His wife sat on her knees on the floor by the cradle, her face turned down, and seemed to sleep breathlessly.

The tailor saw all that while he stole softly to his work place by the window. There an anxious certainty came over him, because he thought his wife had noticed none of it.

"And the work is still lying there where I put it down", he pondered contentedly, since he had in sitting down supported himself with both hands as a precaution and had thereby felt the the pair of old trousers which had fallen from his hand when the illness had befallen his little one.

"Yes, yes", he sighed next and settled into an unhurried dullness.

From the cradle, a soft stirring began, like when a dropped garment is shaken out.

"Haven't you hauled a chair up to him?" his wife asked with pining voice.

She had half risen and held her pale, careworn face towards her husband.

Garbe started gently and swallowed the saliva in his mouth. Then he answered,

"Tine, look, stay quiet! I'm sitting. Don't bother yourself by any means about me."

His wife was offended by this answer and spoke scornfully,

"You, you! — I believe it already. — What is it then: you, I, or all two together! — But he, he ..."

She rose up completely and directed the rigid gaze of her wrought eyes at the dark corner in which Garbe's back lay.

"But he! — He struck out from the mountains over the mountains because I called in my need. You dear Franz, you know it and your Lord and Master who you serve now as angel: like a crumpled beetle in a man's hand, such is my heart!

Pity your mother!

If you won't patter to me anymore then help me at least keep my child here in his room. Bind his soul to his body, for it wants to leave it again and go from me ..."

She spoke it in high, muffled singing tones, in sounds like those the wind creates with the young shoots of leafless trees. And while her exhausted husband was falling sleep in his tailor's chair, his elbows propped on his knees, and let his head sink rocking deeper and deeper, she felt a powerlessness come over her from these imploring words of hers. The torment lessened in her. A dull letting go, the peace of breaking away took possession of her heart. But since the pain was the hand in which she alone carried her child, his fading away created the feeling in her that the dying Heiner was no longer so completely her own. Hastily, but soundlessly, she turned to her child and sought his little hands.

She saw them lying on the covers, thrust out on tense little arms, the little fingers grasped by desire, bent as if they were reaching for something approaching them unseen. At the same time, his little mouth moved as if stuttering words, and the wrinkled little face smiled in awkward beatitude.

"Death is already playing with him", shot through Tine's head.

In fear she grasped after the little hands; but she could not pull them to herself. Drawn away by an invisible force, they constantly slipped away from her trembling fingers.

Then she screamed!

"Heiner, look at me! — Most beautiful child, stay with me!"

The angel of death who had stepped from the corner behind Garbe's back and, standing at the foot of the cradle, had stretched his hand out to his little brother, was overwhelmed by his mother's lament. Heiner's young soul balked at his power and swayed back again entirely into this life.

His little hands lay still like two scattered leaves; the pitiful clatter of his breath became regular, and his eyes quavered animatedly sometimes under their closed lids. Tine took Heiner's little fingers in one hand, rocked the cradle with her foot and hummed a song between her lips so that the child fell asleep.

The drive of her soul after that was so strong that a gentle peace came over her little boy. But the angel of death began again now to let his eternal brilliance work on Heiner's soul. Like the sunlight sucking up drops of dew, imperceptibly, but steadily, so that he shimmered with happiness over his going; that was how he wanted to withdraw his little brother's soul from the vigilant heart of his mother. Then he remembered to hurry away noiselessly with him and thus to evade the snares of human love whose clutches he always felt deeply when he observed his mother's countenance.

But this soul, beaten trembling thin by all the hammers of earthly hardship, had come to such a feeling for outer-worldly things that it was alerted by a strange unrest in her breast before this secret onslaught of the angel of death.

She observed with distrust the silent little face of her child.

The foot of the cradle was arrayed on its upper edge with crude whirls. As the little cot was rocked back and forth under her restless foot, a weak redness came and went from the little clump of light on the table above the pale little head. But that was not what excited Tine's attention so much that the humming between her lips was extinguished; rather she saw a pale radiance sinking over her child, like the shimmer that a white garment throws around itself in the

night. The pale light did not waver if she rocked
the cradle harder; it did not give way if she took a
step back and drew away from the rocking cot.
Then she held one of her emaciated hands over
the little face; only the shadow was not forth-
coming as she expected from her hand. In
anxious astonishment, she finally bent down and
kissed him on the mouth so that his chest would
drink her hot breath; she opened her eyes wide
as if conjuring, pressed the pitiful little body
tightly to her heart, gathered the quite frail life in
her arms and whispered the sweetest, most
foolish terms of endearment.

It was in vain for her to spread the entire
shadow of her need over the child thus. She felt
his soul in her hands, wooed by the glamour of
death, softly gliding away. His shrivelled features
smoothed themselves out in bliss, it was as if the
face was opening up, it became beautiful and
more and more beautiful, like a white flower
slowly opening its calyx to the full moon.

"Look, how beautiful the shimmer of eternity
makes him", the angel of death talked to her
from the middle of her being. "Give it into the lap
of the Lord! Don't begrudge him the eternal light
that heals him for ever, like the morning there
before the window will console you again in your
life."

She saw that the darkness was pressing ever
lighter through the panes over her sleeping

husband whose hunched back half covered the rightmost of the two windows, and realised with horror that her latest child would be taken away by the morning like all the others. Without paying attention to the words of peace in her inner being, she let the child fall into the cradle, threw herself to the floor and raised her hands to heaven.

At the same time, she screamed with crushed voice,

"Garbe! Garbe!! Cover the windows! Don't you see, the day is coming again like a white dog, and when it licks over our child, it will be over with him like with all the others. He is already stiff, cover them tight, Garbe!"

The tailor had seen with the eyes of a deep dream the struggle of his wife with the angel of death, and as she now screamed, the spell of the otherworldliness of his life was not disturbed. He rose with the soundless certainty of a sleep-walker and attached two old miner's coats to the window casements. In the meantime, a long, thin scream carved up the fear of the dull space. It was the voice of Heiner, whom the desperate mother's cry had torn back one last time from his gliding away and flung at the cliffs of life. The tailor shivered within, but twisted again to his cutting table like a sleeping animal and squeezed a heavy groan from his constricted chest.

Tine had sunk down completely and lay on her hands on the floor. Her life had become an empty stupefaction.

With her fingertips, she felt a crack in the floor. She dug her nails into it, and although a splinter of wood drove itself thereby deeper and deeper into the flesh of her index finger, she did not release the grip of her ice-cold hands.

Heiner's flight-lusting soul had torn the scream back from its throat and was torturing the body with spasms so that it would release it: the soul bent it, it did not break, stirred it up so that the skin turned blue and reflective, and turned it over the way laundry is wrung. Tine heard how his limbs kicked against the cradle, now and then a bleating sound. But her heart was not giving up this expiring life. She lay silent and motionless on her hands on the floor and waited.

"Bless your child and release it in peace, then you will have two more hands in heaven to pray for you", the angel of death spoke and his voice shook with emotion. "All life is just shedding; with death we seize ownership of all our treasures", he added subdued.

Tine, as if she had heard that, began to creep on all fours around the cradle, her face turned to the floor; her hair, baked together into strands by sweat, hung over her forehead and dragged across the floorboards. When she arrived at the door, she struck her head dully against its wood and stuttered.

"Why do I never die ... why do I never die ... never and never again, he must stay with me!"

Meanwhile the timepiece of the eternal will made its last strike.

Only the angel of death no longer had the strength to snatch Heiner with violence from his mother. What had frightened him, happened; he submitted to his human love and tumbled to his mother. The glory only glowed like an expiring spark in him, his step became audible, his last earthly clothing, his burial garments, hung on him and skimmed over the floor. And now he stood before her. Then his eternal soul emitted its last call for help, such a terrible groan, as if the entire room was a single tortured human breast.

This sound of superhuman pain tore Tine around. Stunned, she stared at her dead child standing before her in his burial clothes, the corpse's face disfigured by heavenly sorrow into convulsions.

"You have torn me from heaven", he spoke, "now, then take me in your need."

"Franz!"

In blissful horror, his mother raised her arms to draw him to her.

At this moment, the Lord took pity on his angel of death and gave him back his beatitude.

The shadow of his human body sank into the grave to the bones; the waves of his being surged like cheerful fountains back to God, his features became as beautiful as the cloud which passes before the sun; his raiment flowed over his eternal limbs like the white foam of cascading mountain streams, and restrained song lay on his lips.

The eternal conjunction was even accorded in mercy to his mother.

The struggle in her was gone, and she leant with her back to the wall, her head inclined to her breast, and let the blood of her wounded finger drip into the cup of her other hand, because she had not yet apprehended the change in her fate.

"Mother", the angel of death spoke to her with love.

She remained dazed.

"Mother", he repeated once more.

"No, no; my blood still drips, don't call, I must not go with you yet", she finally answered mutely. "But ... but ... for myself ... now; what haven't I endured of everything ..."

"The Lord has turned your feet. Your path runs to your home", he consoled her and she just shook her head unbelievingly at it.

"How often, when my soul had no breath, like now, have I lived it", she spoke after pondering to herself some, then peered into herself and concluded, trailing off, "... and ... nothing happened ...

What are you also saying,, you are far from me ... far ... quite far ..."

"Raise your eyes, mother!"

Tine raised her head with effort and opened wide her still, lacklustre eyes.

"It is dark. The room is like a field and the walls go forth like clouds to all four points of the compass."

The shadow of death ran over her face.

She saw her husband in the darkness as if he was sitting at the end of the world. Mists piled between her and him. She had to go over it to get to him. As she struggled to stride through it, she sank ever deeper, and there was still so much to say.

"Albin", she groaned, "I must go, the end is here, I feel it ... and nobody's going with me ... Heiner!!! —"

"He's going with you", the angel of death comforted her.

"He's going with me ... he's — going — *with* — me —" she repeated in blissful breaths.

Her heart pulled the bell of necessity, and the timepiece of godly will announced her end to the ear of the angel of death.

He faced his mother and closed her senses one after the other.

Under his soft touch, her eyes faded, the hammer of her ears sank down for ever, her tongue went still between her teeth, her breath fell asleep in her nose, and just the skin still twitched for a long time.

Soon her soul stood in the eclipsed house of earthly life in expectation before the gates of death. Deep below her, as though in an abyss, she still heard her heart going in the surges of blood, dull and faint. Finally its beats were also silent, and the trembling of this deepest chamber of life opened the gates of death to her soul.

Heiner's body had also been closed up, and all three stepped out into the mild light flowing towards them. The angel of death in front, the mother behind. But she only took a few steps, then a hesitation came over her. She glanced timidly across the pale expanse before her. She looked humbly over it, her hands clasped low, and shook her head in astonishment.

"Take courage, mother, and walk!" the angel of death encouraged her.

Then she remembered her last child, on whom her God had bestowed the eternal conjunction, and while she turned back, she asked apprehensively,

"Where is my last child?"

But the gates of death in which she looked, searching, were empty. Only a darkness bearing down, mixed with the heavy noise of life, flowed out from it, and the peaceful light of death penetrated over the threshold into the darkness and expired there trembling. No step could be heard.

"Where is my last child?"

Worried, she repeated the question, and since a double-voiced, fine laughter rang out as an answer, she looked back.

But there two thin, beautiful youths stood in white winged vestments, one radiant in eternally steady light, muffling the other's grace so that he looked like a bleached shadow in the pale light. Nowhere did she catch sight of the wasted, little Heiner.

"Don't you recognise your child?" the angel of death asked cheerfully.

Then she knew everything, and since she saw that she had transformed into equally striving beauty like her child, she took courage in her transfiguration and the three sank into each other's arms.

Meanwhile the heavy noises continually penetrated through the open gates of death and disturbed their happiness. The mother wanted to shut the gate, but could not move it.

"The nature of the Lord closes it by itself", the angel of death said. "It is the song of humanity which climbs up the valley of earth to the mountain of life."

The two saved, mother and child, looked down on the angel of death's words more attentively into the grey lying in the depths to which the gates of death led, and soon they heard more than a mere noise penetrating forth: woeful cries of yearning, cutting screams of betrayed love, the dull murmur of hardship, the crying of hungry children, despairing laughter, the voices of raw prayers. It all swelled and sank like bluster of an ocean whose waves drive against the shore. The rare singing tones of pure happiness in it were almost lost to the ear.

The mother turned her timid face to the angel of death and sighed apprehensively.

Suddenly she started as though from a jab to her heart and listened entirely unsettled to the roar of life, though it was ringing out quite far away and indistinctly as if all the wrestlers in the flesh were being torn back by an adverse wave of fate.

Only a tone like the sound of coarse stones being rubbed together by the deep water of rivers, submerged and dulled, reached out of the scattered song of humanity beseeching her heart. The mother did not know who was demanding her, for the memory of her life lay locked in her body below amongst the living. But she was seized by it like the shadow of a forgotten dream besets us, and she shook.

Only the angel of death, the completely purified one, recognised the cry of the tailor who was looking for them with the eyes of a dream.

He took his mother's hand gently and led her away. The stream of certainty flowed from his body into her. The shadow of memory sank in her, and a joy, muffled like the light of her beauty, filled her completely.

Thus the three went through the domain of death down the gentle slope that is called the last descent of life. The shimmering guide in the middle, the mother on the right, his brother on the left.

The air was still and expectation filled it, like those hours brought over the earth which separate night from day. Nowhere was their a source of light, and yet the heights shimmered over their crest in the faint coloured tones of pearl shells. Soft clouds, as though fastened to the same position for aeons, accumulated in this pale brightness merging towards the horizon into a milk-white light. Mountains, far off and in-distinct like intimations of the human soul, towered up in soft lines and assumed in silent play subtle, rare colours: grey, pale violet, golden blond. But no movement at all, no sound at all anywhere in the broad unfolding of this domain. Elysian wistfulness for the end of time.

Thus the immaculately endless region lay there in muffled light. No tree arose, no house; not even the ruined remains of a wall were to be seen. Everything was covered with long, fine grass, May-green, still undisturbed by feet. Only thousands of flowers welled up from the ground in this green endlessness. Here in countless little flakes on stiff thin shrubs like a golden wave washing up; there straight and red like a bloody arrow shot into the dawning white of the distant horizon; scattered blue bells on still stems; large, wonderful flowers, similar to giant butterflies at rest spreading their sparkling wings to the motionless light.

When the mother saw all this beauty around about her, the expectation of eternal youth came so strongly over her that she bent forward to pick these flowers. The joy almost restrained her breath as she braided wreathes for all three from them.

Then they adorned their foreheads, and the dew ran over their faces with each step. And they went then and looked down in front of themselves, for each heard the song in the depths of their being.

The mother broke the silence first.

"How wonderful everything is here!" she spoke in the whisper of fulfillment. "Every stem, every flower stands turned in the direction of our feet and seems to be hurrying to that veil which climbs out of the depths their before us which we are walking towards."

And after a little pondering, she also found the courage to ask about the reason for a peculiar phenomenon which she had already observed for a long time but had deemed too trivial for her children.

On the path which they were taking, namely, modest depressions appeared in the still green like traces of little feet. Sometimes the tips of the grass were barely bent by timid pattering; sometimes impatient, tiny leaps had trodden the stems down.

The mother asked her child, the angel of death, about it.

He raised his arm and pointed out into the distance before them.

"Everything strives for the sea of death which lies there in the depths. To there, on the same path we are walking now, all my brothers and sisters went, and we too must go through the bottomless, blind waters", he said.

The two beautiful shadows walking towards eternity, mother and child, got the better of their trembling and followed the direction of his raised arm with intense eyes.

In the background, in the furthest regions which scooped themselves out like a chasm with gentle slopes, sombre, grave shrouds swelled into the heights, driven straight up by an invisible power of the depths, a heavy, sombre wall, ever moving, but impenetrable, and under it lay the sea of death, a stationary, blue-grey, lustreless surface.

"My children walked through that! — Alone?" the mother asked worried.

"Oh no, an angel led them like I'm leading you. On the shore of the blessed, you will find them all again."

With these words, the angel of death soothed them, and they strained their eyes to penetrate through the shroud before the last mystery. Only the climbing, sombre cloud did not open a crack.

Then the trembling faintheartedness assaulted the mother deeper.

"But if they got lost! I see them all hurrying on the foolish feet of their little bodies, and this one, my child", — with that she pointed to Heiner — "stands in the fullness of his soul before us."

"Mother, your last imperfection is tormenting you. In those waters lying down there, the last shadow from the valley of earth will be washed away from you, and all the hidden sense will then open itself to your eyes."

"Child, and where are the traces of your feet?" she asked and moved closer to him, the angel of death, driven by fright.

He took her in his arms and kissed her cheeks.

"Mother, I was weaned from your breast and had to stride through the door of *my* death. The others all still drank from your heart and therefore had no death of their own, for it grows with life. They went through your last door to their end. Only this brother suffered more than anyone, that's why the fullness of his soul happened before the waters."

While he spoke down to her forehead, he felt how she huddled ever closer to him and always looked back anxiously.

Suddenly she groaned,

"Hold me tighter in your arms! Hold me, child! He is sucking on me!"

"There, there he is!" Heiner cried at the same moment.

The angel of death turned his head.

There he saw something that shocked him too.

Behind them in the blurring distance, the gates of death were yawning open. A few steps from the gates, tumbled into the silent domain, lay Garbe, who in the torment of his being had wandered after them, thrown by the force of the horror onto his chest, staring after them with haggard face, trying always to raise himself and always falling back.

The angel of death's soul shook because of this terrible fate.

With strong arms, he raised his mother and his brother up and fled with them hurriedly to the sea of death.

The swishing of their vestments did not let them hear the scream that Garbe emitted.

Now they had arrived at the shadow wall of the hidden waters.

Garbe saw the sombre shroud torn, and through the gap, the dazzling brilliance sprayed from the mountain of light on which the eternal city shimmers with its golden-green battlements. Eight white vestments hurried down the mountain to the shore of the blessed ... Overwhelming melodies, a ringing storm — it closed in on Garbe, then the haze closed over the blind waters of death again, the dream drained away from him, and the tailor plunged down into the pit of his life again.

His house was completely silent, for homes outlast the life of men.

The red clump of life was still burning peacefully in the lamp as if the light of morning was not there which broke in through the windows next to the miner's jackets and streamed in white strips onto the panes of the pot cupboard.

Mrs Gebeln, who had hurried home to wake her servants, now entered, breathless from her quick walk.

Her eyes, accustomed to the light, were hardly capable of distinguishing much to begin with in the dark room. That's why she paused for a moment on the threshold and listened with concern.

Nothing stirred.

"Now, you still have it dark?" she asked to raise her courage.

When she now also received no answer, she went to the windows to take down the peculiar curtains.

By the cradle, she kicked a pair of boots which had not been thrust aside.

A terrible thought climbed in her.

Fearfully she cried,

"Such a cursed stupidity!" and tore the jackets down.

In the light, all the terribleness was exposed which had occurred in the short time of her being away.

Heiner lay dead in the cradle, a little arm stretched rigidly over the edge as if he was reaching for someone in dying.

Tine, sunk down by the wall next to the door, rested lifeless on the floor, her crossed hands spread pressed against her breast as mothers do who bear away quite small children.

Her corpse's face was fluttering beautifully in the expression of deeply peaceful happiness which filled it.

Garbe lay in between the two on his chest, his face hidden in his hands whose fingers were dug into his temples convulsively.

To start with, she deemed all three to be dead and was overcome by horror.

Then she noticed how the tailor's hand turned to her slipped a little in its pressure, but straight-away drove the fingers energetically again into the yellow skin of his temple so that white rings formed around the nails.

Mrs Gebeln seized him by the collar, shook him and screamed appalled,

"Garbe, get up! Garbe, what are you doing!"

After a few efforts, the tailor got up noise-lessly, sat on the floor, stared at her strangely, looked unknowing and astonished around the room and then lowered his confused glance to his hands whose index fingers he was moving playing next to each other as if he had to think arduously.

"But now, Albin, you've let both of them die!" Mrs Gebeln finally said possessed.

Garbe raised his head and looked at her as if he did not understand what she meant.

Then he looked dully again at his playing fingers.

After a while, his body began to shake more and more powerfully, and tears ran onto his hands. Finally he emitted a howl, threw himself with his chest against the floor again, covered the dirty floorboards with impassioned kisses and stroked them with loving hands. At the same time, he sobbed heartbreakingly.

When Mrs Gebeln began to talk to him, he rose up abruptly and looked at her full of hate.

Suddenly his face transformed to something unrecognisable, a play of quickly racing trans-formations, the faces perhaps of all the events in his life were scurrying over it, and each ossified in it with a part of a trait so that his entire face stared at her finally with an expression of stupid tearfulness.

After a few unsuccessful attempts at speech, it fell from his mouth expressionless,

"Tine, why did you go over the pale field?"

Then he bleated his tongue at her.

Mrs Gebeln recognised that he had gone mad, and drew back to the door. In her fear of death, she talked confusedly, incoherently to him and, at the same time, always held him in her sight, following all his movements with a surreptitious, angry glance.

At the same time, she probably must have enunciated the word money: for he suddenly rushed to the shelf of pots, tore his wallet from a yellow pot, rummaged through the contents counting loudly and then fell down again yammering at the ground.

Mrs Gebeln drew the door shut soundlessly, whilst within the kissing and sobbing of the madman began again.

Then she hurried in flight through the dim courtyard to the street.

The bells of the tower were just then singing over the fields into the clear morning.

The trees rustled with joy in the light. Over the black mountains stood the open gate of the sun.

Its posts dripped with gold.

A flock of white clouds rode inwardly interwoven up to it. They became smaller and smaller and vanished into its radiant depths. The lark's songs accompanied them and their jubilation was lost in the shimmering heavens.

The Tale of the Rustling

The light had slipped from the eyelash of the eternal, and after the long, long darkness, the earth was strolling in the sun's beauty through space. The happy earth enjoyed its young fortune, and the scale of its blessedness grew and developed as a luminous blue circle into the endlessness of space. When the Lord God saw it, he said to himself, "See, now even the earth has its heaven."

The amiable thoughts of the eternal sank down to the earth, and its amenable soil created from it the tender bodies of little plants which spread there leaves out around themselves and then turned their colourful faces to heaven, towards God, without tiring, so long as the night of sleep did not come over the sun. But when the dusk shrouded the light ever tighter, then they laid their little heads on the leaves and waited patiently until the eye of the sun came up again. Then they began anew their silent service. They raised their leaves, which were sweet and white like the little hands of tiny children, and when they turned their faces to it, then their bodies quivered in great joy.

But nothing had a voice in the entire, wide God's earth. Like the smouldering dream of a silent soul, day after day ran from the mountains. The waters streamed soundlessly wave after wave. The shimmering cloth of air hung motionless over the earth, and even the clouds of the heavens changed their subtle colours noiselessly and slipped silently from form to form. That lasted day after day and night after night and did not change. The earth's breath faltered and lay scorching in its secret mouth. The heat of the air climbed, the eye of the sun reddened in its own glow. The clouds of the heavens trembled as though in fever, and when the plants sank their leaves into the waters to cool them, they turned black and withered; for even the waves had turned hot and were going their way with glassy-mad eyes.

"The earth is suffering in its ardency", the eternal vigilance said reflectively to himself. "I will give it a voice so that it will name itself. It should be divided in itself. Its soul will always be between the cry of its mouth and its being."

Thus spoke the Lord God who saw that his peace on earth had become a sickness, rose from his seat, dropped onto the power of his wings and hurried through space. The thunder of his wings filled the universe, and the pillars of its existence shook. The worlds trembled with his flying past like little cocks under the feathers of the eagle. When the wings of the eternal skimmed over the earth, he shook them so that a feather detached itself. It sank down and burrowed down with its tip into the ground that covered the slope of a mountain. Roots ran out at once from it, and it soaked the land with its sap which climbed up and down, and it changed its form according to the laws of earth. Its shimmering shaft became a trunk, hard as stone and rough-looking like the rocks. Its vane, however, transformed itself into a green feather. It raised and lowered itself into thousands of boughs and branches. Before the morning had renewed itself three times, the rustling had become native to the earth which poured its soul into it — its soul which had otherwise lain silent in the depths, its happiness and its sorrow, its laughter and its heavy wisdom, and whensoever the rustling stirred its green wings, it sounded as if the wings of the nameless were skimming past.

Now the first tree had been created, and the air stood around it and heard in astonishment what its green tongue was saying. It was, in that first period already like today, very talkative, and could not keep anything to itself. After the air had listened silently for a while, it burdened itself with as much rustling as it was able to bear, and hurried away to report to its corporeal sisters, the clouds, what new things had happened. They stood remotely in the sky in soundless pallor.

The air climbed ever higher. When the rustling filled the expanses of space, it extended into a great roaring and was barely restrainable anymore. The clouds could not master their shaking, their hearts pounded so violently that they trembled all over. Finally they became completely grey with fright and fled into the heavens. The air screamed at them with all its bodily strength to not be frightened. But the clouds did not want to hear, instead they hurried ever further away without looking around. The sweat just dripped from them and fell in great drops to the earth. In the end, they could flee no more, lay as though slain and fell down exhausted behind the mountains.

The air had meanwhile also lost the rustling. It settled down onto the lowlands ill-temperedly. After some brooding, however, it gathered itself up and was more cheerful than usual; for it had a quite simple soul. While it went here and there, it tested to see if the rustling could be recreated. Only, it pulled itself together so much that it brought nothing forth but a long, indistinct tone. It flew only a little over the blue flowers of broom. Except for the little flowers, only the sun heard it with its ubiquitous rays. The sun was made so tired by the monotonous humming of the air that it forgot to drive away the darkness from its eyes and fell asleep prematurely.

The song of the air also merged slowly into a lullaby. The little plants folded their leaves, which were sweet and white like the little hands of tiny children, bowed their colourful little heads to the side and slumbered too.

Then it was night again, and the blue heavens kept watch alone, high and still. The earth, however, talked uninterrupted with the green rustling that its God had gifted it. It talked everywhere with it, for it had sent out from the first tree little wings which bore in themselves the lively rustling. They flew around everywhere, and when they found a place which seemed good for living, they settled down and grew and rustled like it had to be. Soon all the elevations of the earth had their rustling. The high mountains had a mighty, deep one which rang out roaring; the hills a mild, singing one, and it seemed as though they bore the wings of the wild pigeon circling over its nest. The air, however, still lay across the lowlands and slept, and nobody was there to take the many rustlings and carry them away. Then it flowed down to the ground and gave up its spirit. It turned into a heavy, black shadow trickling down over the mountain.

It came up to the water and fell in. But when it touched the lively waves, it received its spirit again, transformed itself and became what it had been: a cheerful rustling. The waves rejoiced in having a voice too, and let its soul flow into them. The water has a deeper, more manifold inner being than the earth, and its rustling was sometimes a sobbing, sometimes a singing, and sometimes it spoke with the dark, incomprehensible sounds of a primeval depth.

Thus the water carried the rustling from the mountains, further and further into the land and still much, much further. It sparkled and trembled with joy whenever it felt the deep eyes of the heavens resting on it.

From the streams came rivers, from the rivers came torrents. So much rustling accrued in the end that the wandering waters were barely capable of sustaining it. They paused and formed the immeasurable sea. The rustling of the entire earth was deposited over it. Under it the breast of the endless water breathed in quiet deep blows to the rhythm of the stars passing by up above.

Thus it has remained up to the present day of restless humanity. The rustling still sways its feathers over the seas. Whoever hears it, is seized deep in the chest; for the soul knows quite well the wings of its eternal Lord.

The Shadow

Since Johannes Teuber had been pensioned, he had been completely forgotten. He lived in an isolated three room house whose windows looked across the rolling fields to the nearby mountains. In his rooms, such a perfect silence reigned that it occurred to nobody to think that someone lived there. Towards the second half of the morning, he climbed down the stairs with his noiseless step. His hands with his stick behind him, his face bowed in thought, he hurried to the field that he crossed back and forth, pausing from time to time and raking in the earth with his stick, as someone does who cannot come clean with themselves. He must not have been five hundred metres distant, thus he did not look any different in the field from a bare post, he was so thin and delicate. When someone talked to him, he raised his face so and spoke with a young, clear voice about the weather, the path, the harvest or whatever the inquisitive person began the conversation with, and smiled with his overly large eyes so deliberately that nobody tried a second time to take up a conversation with him. Whenever he walked around so aimlessly, in impassioned intercourse with something hidden, he wore the same grey clothes that he had brought over from his time in office, Sunday and weekdays, as if the rest was without meaning for him. He made a quite unreal impression, and hardly had his form vanished from view than it was difficult to imagine it in the flesh: so completely did he seem to be distant from everything that moves the lives of other men.

Nobody could specify exactly when he had come to Weißenhagen. When someone first noticed the little man, how he scurried busily, almost timidly through the heavily populated streets, he had already been living in the place a few years, and nobody was able to specify anything else about him than that he had previously acted as commissioner in Bechtelsdorf and was entirely "without dependents". — —

At one time, still during his time in office, many, many years ago, after the long vacation, he appeared with a quiet, delicate woman on his arm. Assurance lay over his being, his step became firmer and more constant, his eyes saw more freely into the world. But, after how much time, nobody can say, he was walking alone again, yet hastier, quieter and more timid than before. It was said that the quiet, delicate woman was lying at home and dying. She struggled for many moons, seen and guarded by nobody but her quiet, strange husband. Finally he was walking behind her coffin: alone, pale and uncomprehending. With dry eyes, he shook the three little scoops of earth onto her coffin, had a headstone erected on her grave and went away, when he had viewed the work of the stone mason, never to enter the churchyard again. The tomb, a white marble cross, bore nothing but the inscription: Marie Teuber. The women who walked past and read the words, asked bitterly in their hearts how a wife could be buried so lovelessly by her husband and so soon forgotten. Thus it occurred that the pastor of Weißenhagen also became indignant over the hardheartedness of Johannes Teuber, even though, as a christian and teacher, he had to offer in every respect an exemplary front. To remind him of his duty to the dead, he summoned him one day to a severe lecture. When he had concluded his admonitions, Teuber sat silently, his face chalk-white, despairing, his eyes staring fixedly at his thin hands held entwined between his knees. Suddenly he rose up and stepped with raised arms to the writing table before which the pastor was sitting, stuttered something and finally screamed in great torment, "You know nothing at all!" Then he took his hat and went quietly out the door.

The clergyman confessed that it gave him something of a fright when this gentle man sprung towards him, and even hours afterwards, after a dreariness filled his soul as though the misuse of his chaste powers was burdening him. He was henceforward of the opinion that Teuber had been affected, through the suffering and death of his wife, by a nameless misfortune which he was bearing like a hero in a way which proved nothing but that a hard fate makes strange men even stranger. But soon an event would unsettle this mild opinion.

The son of a landowner from the neighbouring village had caught a strong inclination towards the only daughter of a very rich townsman of Weißenhagen, which was returned by the girl who was distinguished just as much by beauty as by a charming spirit. For some while, the pair enjoyed the fretful happiness of a secret love. The yearning to possess the object of his adoration finally overwhelmed the young man and, throwing all caution to the wind, he requested her hand. He was showered with scorn as a "night-lover and dowry-chaser" and, smarting deeply in his manly honour, left the house of the hard-hearted rich people without testing the loyalty of his girl further. The poor girl was deathly sad at seeing herself so easily abandoned, but could do nothing but remain faithful to him in her heart and trust in one of those wonderful coincidences which so often come to the help of unfortunate lovers. Her hopes were in vain. The stars which donate all the loaded consolations were blind to her, and since nobody took pity on her need, she took salvage in the death which had walked day and night next to her for such a long time, until she was willingly led by it one evening through the avenue of lime trees and thrust herself into the pool. On the next day, the lifeless body was dragged to land.

An immeasurable crowd accompanied the lamentable victim of love to her grave, and since the father, a bigoted man, was known to be a benefactor of the school, the teachers sang as a four-part men's choir at her grave. They stood next to the clergyman who intoned with his deep bass the poignant dirge. Johannes Teuber was among them. The pastor's words had released all the pain, and it was *a single* sobbing across the churchyard. Now the bearers stepped to the open grave. The rods on which the coffin had stood over the grave were drawn away and the men grasped the canvas cloths. The singing began, and the dead remains sank falteringly into the earth for ever. In this oppressive moment, as the mother's pain climbed to a distressing lament, Johannes Teuber changed colour in deathly despair. He sought for a moment, flanked by his neighbour, to master the agitation, and he crumpled up the paper in his hands. His thin body shuddered as though there was a heavy frost, and then he fell to the ground with a shrill scream. He thrust his face into the earth and when someone tried to pull him upright, he grasped at the soil with his hands and just groaned, "Martha! Martha! Martha!"

A man from the crowd became furious at this wild outbreak of pain, seized him by the neck, pressed his head into the ground and thus stifled his desperate cries.

Since this time, Johannes Teuber became even shyer. If he had earlier still appeared amongst men on special occasions, he now eschewed them and took to his solitary patrolling in the field and forest. He behaved no differently than if he had compromised his best secret before everyone. But nobody understood his behaviour in the churchyard. With his cry, he could have meant neither his wife nor the dead woman, for both bore other first names, and since it was known that he had manifested at all times the same reserve towards women as towards men, you unfortunately had to abandon the thought of a secret love.

Only it was conceivable that he received in early youth the deep wound of an ill-fated love, carried it all the years silently within himself and now, at the grave of this young victim of the most beautiful human passion, had been shocked into unconsciousness by the memory.

This enlightenment occurred first to a teaching colleague who had worked at the same school as Johannes Teuber. He delighted in it as a result of an innate instinct which evokes in everyone the strong interest in the life of others where fragile relationships are manifested. But there were no deeper reasons which beguiled him into directing his sharp eyes searchingly at the sorrow of men, rather the baser joys alone prodded him to the discovery of a scandal. For that he possessed energy and patience enough to follow his suspicion steadfastly through a confusion of contradictory occurrences. This man whom the constant agitation of his gleeful soul had prematurely turned grey set about making enquiries about Teuber's family, his life during his studies and above all about the circle of acquaintances during his time in Bechtelsdorf. He reaped a quite large harvest and revealed that the life trajectory of Johannes Teuber had proceeded as steadily as is only bestowed on a man from very narrow circumstances, who cannot suppress the ambition of bestriding the lectern of a primary school. In addition, this criminologist had a disposition to gauge everything too much according to outward signs. Consequently the fact only received attention as a suspicious appearance before his nose that Johannes Teuber had stood in quite close association in Bechtelsdorf with the then senior commissioner, Müller, who as a profligate and ill-natured daredevil had been almost completely isolated socially. Suddenly, without apparent cause, Johannes Teuber had backed away from the landowner and quit his position as an official. Right at this time, the solitary daughter, who as a slim, melancholy beauty was still in the memory of all Bechtelsdorf residents, had disappeared to not long after become the better half of the director of a sugar refinery in a distant province.

It was bold to think of the possibility of a love affair between a teacher and the daughter of a great agriculturalist, even downright grotesque when you imagined this timid, thin little man whose entire power lay in his large eyes. Only the young woman had been called Martha Müller, and that was the single point which did not leave the scout completely in despair of arriving at the small man's secret.

With an assurance, which he obtained in the blink of an eye, in which his gift for composition had become serious, he surprised Johannes Teuber on his isolated strip and began to talk about a fabricated journey on which all kinds of extraordinary things would have happened to him. Thus he also met at the station of Thale in Harz with a retired estate owner, named Müller, who administered to his needs in a selfless way as a fine, gracious cavalier, since he, unused to travel, had lost his luggage. Now he slipped ever closer, told also of his daughter and her husband, a needlessly pompous man, and observed attentively, walking next to the little man, his face and gestures.

Teuber listened calmly, stabbed his stick deep into the ground now and then and, in a pause which the speaker had to allow because his imagination had run out, raised his face, riveted his eyes on him and said with gentle resolve, "Yes, there you have correctly found things out for sure; a senior official named Müller was on the estate in Bechtelsdorf during my time there. His daughter also bore the name Martha, exactly the same as I named in my nervous shock at the churchyard. — — But, I ask you, is that a disgrace?"

Then he shook his head with an angry laugh, placed his stick behind his back and lapsed into meditative reclusion.

This self-absorption lay like a fog around him so that the interrogator, having failed to make any inner contact with him, emitted a flood of apologies and reassurances, lost himself in banal wordiness and finally went from him with the feeling that he had been very stupid, but also in the dogged belief that something must have occurred between Johannes Teuber and Martha Müller.

And while he strode the stony path to the village, he still saw the poignantly large eyes of the little teacher directed at him and had to bear out the pastor's opinion that a quiet obsession resided in them. God, and if they had made an impression on him, why should it be so entirely impossible that they had not turned dangerous for a young, silly thing, especially in their youth when their penetrating glow had certainly smouldered more powerfully than today. Such pondering drove the unsuccessful inquisitor into ever quicker stumbling. He wanted to oppose it with his will so crossly that it seemed as if he was fleeing.

If he had been marked with the fine impressibility of the nervous, he would have probably felt on his back the bitterly mocking glance of Johannes Teuber. For the little man was standing on the edge of the forest and following with his eyes the man stumbling away. He placed an angry, wounding power in his eyes, a power with which he drove him to flight, and it seemed as if he was exhausting himself with this rigidly hostile look, for the expression of his face became more and more empty. It paled and finally solidified into that desperate wistfulness which is the shadow of sombre, sleepless memories. He had been thrust by the crude curiosity of his colleague into the midst of the hidden maelstrom of his life. The fever from the ravines of his past overwhelmed him. In vain he broke out into loud laughter to shake it off; in vain he began to run hurriedly to diminish his misery from without: it seemed again as if the smouldering incubus was sitting on him and wanting to ride him to his death. In the evening, he returned to his residence under the shelter of darkness pale and exhausted, his clothing besmirched, dotted with wispy needles and the hair-thin grass of the forest clearings, as if he had been wrestled down by an opponent in battle and dragged across the ground. His dolefully fat housekeeper emitted a cry of fright. Teuber, whose head was hanging back like that of a drunkard, laughed hoarsely at the ceiling as he entered. Slurring to himself, "I want nothing to eat, nothing, nothing at all", he brandished his hat dodderingly and vanished into his room, drawing the door firmly shut behind himself.

Mrs Nossig heard his stick banging over the floorboards and the grating of his armchair, listened to a few more groaning breaths and then took to her chair between the kitchen cupboard and sideboard to fathom out what circumstances could have brought the honourable man to such a deep, sinful state. For that the hairnet of wine fumes hovered over him could not be denied. In her eagerness to discover amongst the looser menfolk of the place the culprit who could have misused the artlessness of this solitary child's soul for his amusement, she fell ever deeper into the region of worldly disgracefulness and indulged with passion these sorry meditations until, shoving her wrung hands carefully under her head, she lay down to blessed sleep. She awoke deep in the night. Soft rasping breaths were coming from Teuber's room. Mrs Nossig crept noiselessly in to ascertain if her help was perhaps still needed.

The blinds had not been let down, the bed was untouched, the room was filled by the hazy light of the full moon, a light in which an unease lay. The milky light was driven by weak pulses trembling against the walls so that all the objects seemed to float to and fro as though under flooding waves of water. Finally she spotted Teuber still in the armchair which he had obviously not left the whole time.

His thin body hung stretched out on the outermost edge of the seat, and he was holding his face turned motionless towards the woman entering like he was paralysed by an unexpected occurrence between shock and panic.

When Mrs Nossig went to take another step forwards, Teuber stretched out his right hand towards her dismissively and said with infinitely sad voice, "Marie, you know it! Don't come nearer, she still blossoms over me, stronger and livelier than ever." Mrs Nossig, whose first name was Alma, saw well that she was not intended, and thought it involved hallucinations here like those an overdose of alcohol straightaway created in complete teetotallers. But his voice! His voice was so oddly clear and certain!

With that she pulled herself together and said, "Sir, it is deep into the night ..."

But she had to break off, for her words sounded both stupid and unreal at the same time to her, spoken by the voice of a stranger with a hot mouth into her ear, and Teuber had stretched out even more. All of him, his un-engaged face, his wide-open eyes, his mouth, was a morbidly tense listening.

"Keep talking", he said and swallowed audibly in anxious expectation.

Since she did not comply from fear of his demand, he lowered his head disappointedly and looked at his hands entwined between his knees. Mrs Nossig used this favourable moment and slunk back from the full light of the moon into the darkness to escape in its shelter. She was just raising her hand to the door handle when Teuber's voice became loud again.

Still bowed over his hands, he said in bitter accusal,

"Lord, always the Lord!"

Then he lifted his face, drilled his glance at the place she had just left, and asked surreptitiously that being with whom he had confused his housekeeper, his dead wife whose spirit he believed he had before him, "Yes, why does the Lord not like you, since you are with him nevertheless? — Or, why don't you stay with him, rather than hound my days so that they run before me like dogs with glassy eyes? And my nights, my nights, which nevertheless aren't mine? ... The Lord, hmhm, — Go and complain to him that you would die next to me a second time, if you must live next to me a second time."

Suddenly he was straightening up and talking sharply and precipitately to the old position,

"Why don't you stay in the residences behind the grave! No, in heaven, you were not my wife!! I did not touch you, neither with my body nor my soul! And if you died of it then it was your fault since you expected from me what I must not give you as long as your image, your beautiful shadow, beautiful, sweet as your life, blossomed over me day and night!"

With the last words, he raised his face slowly to the ceiling and remained thus with a misty-eyed look as if he had succeeded in scaring away the inimical shadow, and as if the longed for image was now shimmering nearer. During this reverie by the unfortunate man, Mrs Nossig succeeded in slipping out of the room unnoticed. But before she could find in the darkness on the kitchen table amidst the crockery the key to her bedroom, Teuber's voice rang out again from the adjoining room. It seemed sometimes to come from the back corner, sometimes she heard him speaking hard at the door. He must thus have been wandering soundlessly in the room or, remaining in the same position, turning sometimes here, sometimes there. In any case, he had calmed down. His words flowed easily with the accustomed mild voice. Only now and then did they become disturbed by something like a stifled sobbing. And since female curiosity is always stronger then fear, this sound drew Mrs Nossig's ear to the door again. He must have been walking about the room, for she heard quite clearly the words, "Everything would jump that lies and withers in me. Oh, everything, everything would be forgotten."

After that it was dead silent. She heard the crunching of her ankles as she stepped back from the door and thought, 'now he has thrown himself dressed onto his bed and will soon be asleep.' Against expectation he began stammering unintelligibly: with flaring ardency, in torment, disordered, jubilant, like the ageing woman had only enjoyed once in her youth, and always penetrating out of the confused flow was a cry in extreme ecstasy which she could not understand. It sounded like wha, har or Martha. But every time the image of a youth formed before her soul, a youth who hurried in the smouldering midday sun's scorching course and brandished a blossoming branch over his head in ecstasy.

Now more than ever full of fear — for what might happen if he came out and found her! — she fled to bed in her innocence.

The next day, she asked for her release, as her mother was sick and needed her care. Teuber's face was pale and tired out. His eyes lay like two great blue wounds beneath his forehead. He nodded in agreement and smiled with infinite sadness when in farewell he laid his fine, ever softly trembling hand in her well-upholstered old organ.

"I wish your mother heartily a speedy recovery and thank you for your faithful service", he said and looked up at the same time with such a deeply serious look that, out of inexplicable shyness, she did not dare to speak in Weißen-hagen explicitly about the reason for her sudden departure. Nevertheless the rumour emerged in the village after some time that Johannes Teuber had murdered his wife, this angel of goodness and beauty, over a secret love affair. Those especially who had become furious over his incomprehensibly raw behaviour after the blessed woman's death brought public opinion for a while into passionate indignation.

He whom it concerned probably learnt nothing of this agitation. For Johannes Teuber was already living now as a hermit in the isolated house. After the sudden departure of good Mrs Nossig, a rapid decline in his powers set in. His sleep gave way to a feverish half-slumber, his rest looked like apathy, his cheerfulness like fury. His memory was partially extinguished, and on the way home from the school, he paused in the middle of the flooding traffic, looked around anxiously and then went into a stranger's house. In class he endangered the children entrusted to him with sudden outbreaks of violence. The fury rampaged in him until he sank apathetically into his chair. Thus the authorities decided on his retirement.

You have probably worked a lot at nights and not conserved your powers at school?" the examining doctor asked him and added as an incorrigible philosopher, "For good, healthy flesh preserves itself."

Johannes Teuber raised his lowered gaze and answered with a painfully happy smile,

"Yes, Doctor, many a beautiful night. Oh, how how many. It is probably from that. But I won't reproach myself, for exhaustion also means hollowing out."

"Yes, but you only have one life", was the response of the doctor who set himself ready for a debate from which many an instructive fact over psychopathy was to be obtained.

"For that reason alone, I am not sad", Teuber answered simply and endorsed it himself. Thus it went.

From now on, the prematurely aged man constantly wore a bright shimmer on his face, as if he was always walking by a white wall, and there always lay in his eyes a deep astonishment over an indecipherable dream. In that first year after his redundancy, his enemies also endeavoured to find by all means the reason why, rambling in the field, he talked to himself and, in this gesture of helplessness, rooted about in the soil with the tip of his stick. After many oscillations, the view came through: as penalty for the crime against his wife, God had taken his sanity and he must now dig for the dead where he stood or walked. No impartial person, however, on whom the wonder of these beautiful, aged eyes had rested believed these malicious ideas.

Only quite sharp observers noticed at the time a colourless ring around his pupils, dull and lifeless, which looked like the beginnings of blindness. With the passing of years, this blanching grew ever wider until finally in the place of the soul-deep blue, a milky, opalescent disc swam in the aged-yellow white of the eyes. It took twenty years until the shimmer of his eyes was seared from within, they were rigid, seemingly without sight, really like those of the blind. Nevertheless his vision had forfeited nothing. For as usual, the tiny man was seen in the fields, only somewhat more bowed and unsteady. Only he did not dig with his stick for the dead anymore, but held his bleached eyes in never tiring expectation towards the endless distance, while he was walking about. If somebody spoke to him then he waved them off with an impassioned gesture and walked away from them listening. From peaks far off beyond all the mountains, the voices must have set off for him, voices whose drawing near only his riveted eyes perceived.

On many a spring night, they sounded much stronger to him. Then he answered them. He was heard singing a gentle, sweet song in the middle of the night. The young daughters of the house-keeper, sleeping beneath his room, thought it sounded, as strange as it also was, like the song of a lover, and they would be seized each time by such a trembling that they had to hug and kiss each other in tears.

In the winter of his seventy-first year, Johannes Teuber discontinued his customary walk completely and spent the days at that window from which the passing trains could be seen. He did not neglect to examine attentively every train coming from the Grafschaft Glatz, as if he expected the arrival of a person dear to him. In the intervening period, he leafed eagerly through the yellow timetable like someone planning a long journey and even spread all his old tickets out in front of himself. Staring raptly at them, his increasingly impatient soul travelled all over the world. Thus the winter passed.

One day his new housekeeper heard him leave his bed earlier than usual. With a commotion and a rumbling about that she had never known with him, he dressed and appeared soon after on the threshold in his archaic black festive clothes, asking with determined voice, to the nervous astonishment of the housekeeper, whether a letter had arrived. Despite the negative response, he nevertheless left the house brushed up, his tall hat on his white hair, the never used stick with the silver hook in his hand.

After he had bought a brace of red roses in a flower shop, he struck off on the path to the railway station and strode back and forth on the platform with unease, peering down the tracks. The train roared thundering under the roof of the platform, the doors were torn open, and the travellers streamed out. Teuber, holding the flowers high in comical anxiety with a continual "sorry", elbowed his way fiercely through the swarm. If he caught sight of an old woman then he hesitated for a moment, took a small step to speak to her, and desisted sadly when he noticed that it was not the hoped-for one. Before the resumption of their journey, he examined again the faces of the passengers leaning out and then threw the roses onto the tracks where they would soon be destroyed by the wheels. Lastly he stood for a long time and stared after the wagons hurrying away until he pulled himself out of his meditations, glanced around self-consciously and went away coughing discretely.

It was repeated now in that manner every day to the enjoyment of the railway officials. Sometimes the comical old man appeared in the morning, sometimes towards evening. But the scene always played out before the carriages of the mountain train.

After he had battled through the travel mix-ups of July, his exhaustion was unmistakable. From now on after entering the platform, he took a seat on the bench next to the exit and, resting the inevitable brace of roses on his knees, he often examined the stream of humanity with the air of final desperation. Only no sentiment, no request, brought him to relinquish his incomprehensible drive. To everything he had as an answer the smile of those who know their success is certain.

Perhaps his last experience was also really the fulfillment of his last hope.

It was in August of the same year, on a day in which a suspicion of the nearby autumn attacks this dazzling month. The white sunlight lay as though having moved fleeing into quite distant parts. Shimmering haze flowed around all things so that they stood there without shadows. The railway station building lay there vast and rapt, and the people going in and out were shouting unnecessarily loudly in their struggle against the pressure which weighed on all of them and was only increased by the oppressive stillness.

Johannes Teuber, who on this day had to stop
on his accustomed path more often than usual,
had just lapsed into impassive cowering after he
had taken his seat on the bench. The brace of
roses lay next to him on the slats of the seat, and
he was holding his hands constantly between his
knees, their palms fitted together precisely. In
the gap, he only moved his index fingers against
each other and shook his white head negatively.
Even when the expected train was hesitantly
arriving, he did not change his posture. Only a
few doors opened, and the few travellers hurried
across the lonely place as though fleeing.

Lastly an old lady stepped from the second
class compartment. While the bearer of her
luggage made for the long distance train departing in fifteen minutes from the other platform,
she steered her steps to the roofed part of the
platform to walk in the mild light there. She had
a slim figure with a beautiful, peaceful face. The
welling crest of her rich, platinum hair in
combination with her young eyes lent her an
almost girl-like charm. Hardly had she carried
her harmonious gait ten steps in the direction of
old Teuber than the poor old man started from
his lethargy, bowed his head for a moment of
short hesitation, gathering himself, and then
stood up, solemnly erect, the tall hat in his hand,
in front of the lady who, be it from surprise over
the audacity of a total unknown, be it in first

shock of recall, started a little and looked as a precaution to the station building in whose open door an assistant was leaning. He understood her questioning look and stroked his forehead with a smile to indicate that it involved a man with a good-natured temper. Then he withdrew through the telegraph room into the little waiting room which, tucked into the space, provided a comfortable listening post. Hardly had he slunk into the corner there than they were both walking over to Teuber's bench. The little old man's face was pale with mortal happiness. The lady took a seat and Teuber remained standing next to her throughout while he spoke confusedly in great excitement.

"But why, sir, do you not prefer to sit?" the stranger asked him a second time.

"Martha, why are you saying 'sir' to me?" Teuber asked dismayed again, held his head bowed for a while and then quickly sat down next to her. After some pondering whilst looking at his hands, he continued,

"Have you been happy, Martha?"

"Not always."

"And now?"

"I am an old woman. — And you?"

Teuber looked at her full of grievous reproach, then he answered hesitantly,

"I have been a flame saved for this moment. I lived for nothing but these minutes when my lips could tremble before you. I knew, oh, I knew quite exactly that I would not die before I had seen you once more."

The lady made a movement to rise.

"Do you want to stand up so over hastily now too like in the arbour in Bechtelsdorf, and break what must now be gone for all eternity?"

The stranger laid her fingers on his shaking hand and reminded him tenderly, "Don't get upset!"

Struggling in vain against the frisson which this touch brought over him, he stammered,

"Yes. But I would not have been for fifty years the stone which was always thrown and always burst asunder and yet was never destroyed ..."

"What are you saying?"

"Johannes, say Johannes to me, Martha, just once for God's sake!" he implored in extreme agitation.

"What are you saying to me, Johannes?" the stranger asked in pitying obedience. After a short hesitation, Teuber answered arduously, "Because your father made this affront to me then and struck me in the face ...", he then sat and spoke the rest silently with discoloured lips until his words became loud again. "But my hand and my mouth were forbidden revenge because of you and later too because of your children. Your reputation was holier to me than my life."

"Are you married, Johannes, and do you rejoice over your children?" the stranger asked, guiding him on gently.

"Oh, I was bound, but not married. She walked next to me and did not become my wife. She died from you, who visited me every night —." The old man grasped the lady's hands and covered them with feverish kisses.

With a start, the beautiful woman broke free and disappeared breathing heavily to the railway station gates from which the bell for departures was sounding. Teuber made a few vain attempts to rise too. But he was soon sitting silently with his head hanging low, his face turned towards the pale, fleeing light of the heavens.

When the assistant stepped out after the dispatch of the train, he found a dead man with an expression of extreme happiness in his face and open eyes.

Johannes Teuber also had to be buried with open eyes because his eyelids had frozen apart.

About the Publisher

Our mission is to provide translations into English of the complete works of neglected major European writers. We do not cherry-pick works that seem the most marketable, but rather seek to provide a complete collection of each writer's works so that readers can follow the writer's development and decide on its merits for themselves.

http://www.facebook.com/KANitzPublishing